Eternal Kiss

Also by Anastasia Dubois

A SLAVE TO HIS KISS

Eternal Kiss

Anastasia Dubois

LIBRIS

An *X Libris* Book

First published by X Libris in 1996

A CIP catalogue for this book
is available from the British Library.

ISBN 0 7515 1728 3

Photoset in North Wales by
Derek Doyle & Associates, Mold, Clwyd
Printed and bound in Great Britain by
Clays Ltd, St Ives plc

X Libris
A Division of
Little, Brown and Company (UK)
Brettenham House
Lancaster Place
London WC2E 7EN

Prologue

A HOT, DUSTY wind swept across the plains of southern France, parching the dry land and making the leaves rattle on the vines like old bones.

Esteban stood by the window, watching the first glimmerings of dawn coming up over the sea. He was not alone, but loneliness ached within him like an empty darkness. Seven hundred years of loneliness.

The restless loneliness of the vampire.

He turned and looked at the girl in the bed. She was beautiful enough. Her golden skin seemed to shimmer against the white satin sheet which fell carelessly across her body, baring one small and perfect breast. The pink rosebud of her nipple was still pert and hard from the savagery of his kisses. As he watched, she stirred in her sleep, turning onto her side so that her long dark hair fell onto the pillow, baring the smooth sweep of her throat.

Esteban averted his eyes, suddenly ashamed. He bitterly resented the dark need which, from time to time, he was driven to satisfy. The tiny punctures on the girl's neck would have healed before the sun rose over Valazur, and she would remember nothing of their night of frenzied passion. On this occasion he had been careful, restrained even; had made sure not to drink too deeply of her sweetness. This one would live on – and so must he. But what was this life but a living death, when he must live without the only woman he had ever cared for?

The Englishwoman filled his thoughts, his dreams, each never-ending moment, with a torment so sweet that he did not even want it to end. Venetia. Venetia . . . He loved her, he hated her, he could have destroyed her and made her his for ever; but on some insane, altruistic whim he had set her free and now he must live with that folly for all eternity.

Pushing open the window, he threw back his head and closed his grey eyes, letting the hot rush of air buffet his face. Behind him, the girl sighed in her sleep, and the hunger stirred briefly within him. But he did not go to her. He would be strong. He *must* resist the darkness or it would engulf him utterly, devouring the last vestiges of his humanity.

Turning, he walked swiftly out of the room and into the cool, comforting darkness of his ancient house.

Chapter One

WITH A KICK of her heels, Venetia Fellowes cut a
graceful arc through the shimmering blue water.
Its coolness felt indescribably good on her skin
after the blazing heat of the Mediterranean sun.

Behind her sped the muscular shape of
Demetrios, the Greek graduate student who had
been occupying so much of her time since she
came to join a multi-national team working on a
variety of archaeological projects on the island of
Malta.

Oxygen hissed into her mouth from the scuba
tank. She could scarcely breathe for giggling as
Demetrios reached out to grab her, and she
wriggled neatly out of his grasp, speeding on
through the water towards the sunken ruins of
the ancient settlement.

It was a strange, eerie place, thought Venetia as
she swam between the broken towers of what
had once been a citadel, now home to shoals of
tiny, many-coloured fish. How old was it – four
thousand years? Five? And what cataclysm had
destroyed the settlement, plunging it beneath the

warm, turquoise-blue waters? In her mind, Venetia could hear whispering voices, the voices of the people who had one lived here, worshipped here, fought and made love. Excitement made her skin tingle. There were so many secrets still to be unravelled, and she felt so good – so . . . so very alive.

Venetia had felt a powerful attraction to the project from the moment she first heard about it. Maltese history fascinated her, with its lost civilisations, its tantalising legends, its mysteries; and as an expert in deciphering ancient languages, she had been taken on immediately by the project's director, Dr Marcus Hale.

She caught sight of Demetrios out of the corner of her eye; lying in wait for her behind a broken and crumbling wall, the water between them glittering with shoals of tiny, coloured fish. This time she wasn't quick enough to escape him and his hands closed about her, drawing her close against his strong, well-muscled body.

Venetia wriggled deliciously in his embrace; not seriously wanting him to let go, only wanting to prolong the pleasure of the chase. He shook his head. No, he wasn't going to let her go, not this time. She raised her eyebrows: what, here? He understood and nodded. Yes, here. Why not here? Who's to see . . .?

Who but the ghosts?

Taking her mouthpiece from between her lips, Demetrios forced a kiss on her mouth. It was all bubbles and fumbling, the kiss half-choking her as she laughed and took in a mouthful of seawater. But it excited her to feel him forcing his passion on her, holding her very tightly as they tumbled over and over among the ruins.

The sightless eyes of fallen statues watched them play, rolling in the water like seals, their bodies sleek, perfectly matched.

At last Demetrios gave her back the mouthpiece and she sucked in the oxygen greedily, fighting to get her breath back through the laughter. Not that Demetrios was giving her a chance to recover. He was making love to her, making her pulse race with pleasurable anticipation as his hands slipped underneath the cups of her red bikini and squeezed her willing breasts.

She writhed, serpent-like in his embrace. Bad boy; bad, bad boy, she felt like purring, scratching, growling. Do it to me; do it again and again.

The thought that, at any moment, other members of the diving team might discover them only added to the thrill of the moment. With each movement of her body, the water lavished new caresses on her, sliding between her thighs, over the firm hummocks of her breasts, the generous swell of her buttocks and the secret valley between . . .

Oh yes, yes, yes. Venetia found herself instinctively responding to her Greek lover's knowing caresses. Not that she was under any illusions about their relationship: it was about raw physical attraction, and that was all there was to it. Both of them knew that, once the project was over, they would walk out of each other's lives – and that unspoken understanding made their coupling all the more intense.

Venetia's nipples were turning into hard little hazelnuts under Demetrios's caresses. He rubbed them with a circular motion, his palms moving round and round over their tips; not too hard, just enough to drive her crazy. Reflexively, her thighs parted, welcoming the intrusion of his leg, rubbing gently against her mount of Venus.

They did not need to speak or kiss. Their mutual need was powerfully expressed in their eyes, their caresses. Treading water, Venetia slid her hands down her lover's flanks, feeling the firmness of muscle beneath tanned skin. Her fingers slid down over his buttocks and thighs, then moved slowly and seductively forwards until they were grazing the swell of his balls, taut and firm beneath the tight wet fabric.

Demetrios was a work of art; like a living statue, perfectly proportioned in every way. And his manhood never failed to excite her. It rose up like some hard, ripe stamen arching above the twin, heavy seed-pods of his testicles. Savouring every moment, Venetia let her fingertip roam up along the hard swell of his dick, enjoying the answering shudder of pleasure which ran through him as she teased the bare dome of his glans, pushing its way out from under the waistband of his trunks.

Still Demetrios was one move ahead of her. Taking hold of her hand, he used it to ease his trunks down over his manhood, letting it spring free, and a dart of passion arched towards the aching need between Venetia's thighs.

His thigh worked its way a little deeper between hers now, easing and insinuating itself against the warm, pulsing softness of her sex. Her back was against a heap of broken stones, half-covered with vivid, feathery fronds of green, and the red mouths of sea anemones, opening and closing with a hunger Venetia's body echoed joyfully.

He pushed her softly against the wall, happy that she was his utterly, his to do with as he chose. And he chose to give her pleasure, his thigh moving away only to allow room for his fingers to slide down Venetia's bikini bottom.

She offered no resistance as they slid down onto her thighs, the stretchy material easily giving way so that she could part her legs still wider and admit the probing tips of Demetrios's fingers.

Venetia wanted to scream out loud, her breath halting and hoarse. She offered herself shamelessly, ravenously to her lover, opening herself up so that there could be no more secrets between them. His shaft was between her fingers, sliding wetly back and forth, the pinkish-purple of his glans like some luscious sea-creature, predatory and seductive, luring her in only to devour her.

Suddenly Demetrios seized hold of her more tightly, pulling himself against her so that she gave a muffled cry. Behind his face-mask, his eyes were sparkling with lust. She did not need words to know what was in his mind. He thrust his hips forward, and the love-dart of his penis sought out the hot, wet heart of her sex with ruthless accuracy, scything into her, embedding itself within her softness.

And in a moment they were one. Moving together, coupling like beasts possessed by the ancient, bacchanalian spirits which had once danced in festivals through these ancient, sunken streets. Around them fish wove patterns of silent wonder: groupers, amberjack, flying gurnard, scorpion fish . . .

Venetia thrilled to the sensations rippling through her as Demetrios penetrated her, his strong hips thrusting against hers, flesh against flesh, bone grinding against bone. It felt so good that she wanted it to go on for ever; and yet she knew that this electric thrill could not last long. It was too sudden, too powerful; a sword-thrust of pleasure which would depart as quickly as it had come.

Hungrily they plundered each other's bodies, pawing and clutching at willing flesh, the sweat of their lust licked away by the gently-swirling waters which enfolded them. And Venetia felt the ocean-swell of orgasm building up inside her, at first quite far away, like waves on a distant beach; then closer and closer, a white, foam-crested breaker crashing down upon her, until she was no more than a tiny presence at the heart of a great bow-wave of pleasure.

As the feelings ebbed away, Demetrios and Venetia loosened their grip on each other, but they did not part. They looked at each other, their eyes expressing what their tongues could not.

More. They wanted more. This first coupling had been nothing but a beginning, an appetising taste of the pleasures which their young and eager bodies craved.

Taking her by the hand, Demetrios kicked out and began swimming towards the surface. Venetia knew where he was leading her. Just around the headland from the expedition's headquarters lay a tiny cove, completely cut off from the rest of the island by steep cliffs, accessible only from the sea.

The sand there was pure gold, soft as a feather bed and – at this time of the morning – warm as a lover's embrace.

Venetia shivered with anticipation as they broke the surface and swam together towards the welcoming beach. She loved her work, of course she did. She also knew that at this moment, she and Demetrios were supposed to be on the road to Paola, heading out to help the team excavate a Roman temple near the hypogeum. They'd get there eventually, she told herself; the site was an important one and she was looking forward to the challenge. But some things were more important even than work.

Sometimes, the only thing that really mattered was pleasure.

'Venetia.'

Slinging a towel around her shoulders, Venetia turned round. Marcus Hale was standing in the doorway to his office, arms folded. She knew what he was thinking, and he was right. But she didn't feel guilty – well, not *very*.

'You wanted something?'

'Come inside, I want a word with you.'

He gestured her into the office and, somewhat reluctantly, she followed him inside. It was hot, stifling, despite the air-conditioning fan toiling round and round on the ceiling. Outside, the sapphire sea off Marsaxlokk sparkled and enticed, dotted with brightly-painted fishing boats and the occasional motor cruiser. This was definitely not a day for being indoors.

Marcus sat down at his desk and Venetia sat opposite, crossing her long, slim legs at the ankle.

She knew she looked good in shorts, but Marcus was oblivious to any charms she might or might not have, and Marcus's clean-cut, English gentleman image left her stone-cold. Right from the word go there had been a faint, unspoken antipathy between them. Venetia had often been criticised for thinking of nothing but work, but compared to Marcus she was a *Baywatch* bimbo. As far as Marcus Hale was concerned, nothing existed beyond The Project.

'Where were you this morning?' he asked coolly. Venetia noticed the slight hesitancy in his voice, as though he wasn't sure he wanted to hear the answer. It was a fair bet that he didn't. Everyone knew what a prude Marcus was.

'I drove over to Paola. You asked me to take a look at the temple inscriptions, remember?'

Marcus gave a curt nod, then fiddled with his pencil.

'And Demetrios? You took him with you?'

'He's my assistant, Marcus. What am I supposed to do, lock him in a cupboard all day?'

'Ah yes, your personal assistant.' Marcus's thin lips twitched into a half-smile, then banished it. 'It's amazing how broad a job description can be.'

A faint rush of anger quickened inside Venetia.

'What's that supposed to mean?'

'Whatever you think it means.' He leaned across the desk and fixed Venetia with a hard stare. 'Look, Venetia, you're a brilliant archaeologist, I'm not disputing that. I'm just not sure you're taking this project seriously enough.'

Venetia returned his stare with a raised eyebrow.

'You're accusing me of not doing my work?'

Hale had the decency to squirm a little. He wasn't good at people. He was better with rocks.

'Well, I didn't exactly say . . .'

'Then what, *exactly*?'

The project director cleared his throat.

'Those preliminary drawings. I need them by tomorrow at the latest.'

Venetia reached into the attaché case by her chair and took out a slim sheaf of papers. She pushed them across the desk.

'These, you mean?'

Marcus picked them up and leafed through them. Venetia could feel his disappointment. They were very thorough. Impressive even.

'Er . . . yes.'

'They're satisfactory?'

'They seem to be.'

'Good. Oh, and I prepared that report you wanted for our submission to the Maltese government.' She added it to the pile. 'Now, perhaps I can go and get some *pastizzi* and a glass of wine? I haven't eaten since breakfast.'

She half got up out of her chair, but Marcus called her back with a snap of his fingers. It really irritated her when he did that – made her feel more like a barmaid than an archaeologist.

'Is there something else?'

'Tonight's presentation.' Marcus gave a sigh and sank back into his chair. 'Let's not fight about this, Venetia. We're supposed to be on the same side. I thought you cared as much about this project as I do. That's why I was so keen to take you on.'

'Don't bullshit me, Marcus – you can't deny my commitment. I've been working eighteen hours a day to get this up and running.'

11

'I know, I know.' He smoothed his mid-brown hair back from his high forehead. It was moist with sweat, his hair hanging limply. Venetia thought he looked slightly pathetic. 'But we've run into trouble. Big financial trouble. The Americans have pulled out, and if we don't get more funding pretty damn quick, we won't have the cash to carry on.'

'It's really that bad?'

'Why do you think the local workers haven't been paid for a fortnight? It's hand to mouth, Venetia.'

'I'm sorry, I didn't realise.'

'You weren't supposed to. Once the vultures know we're down, they'll be in for the kill.' Marcus folded his hands and glanced out of the window, towards the quayside where a group of local labourers were cleaning and labelling artefacts raised from the sunken citadel. 'The thing is, this presentation tonight . . . it's mainly for the benefit of a guy called Gabriel Engelhart.'

Ventia shrugged.

'Never heard of him.'

'Neither had I until the day before yesterday. But it seems he's a billionaire art dealer – more money than he knows what to do with, apparently. So if we can really impress the guy, maybe – just maybe – we can persuade him to invest some of it in this project.'

'And you think I can influence him somehow?'

'You're the great communicator, Venetia, not me. I'm terrific with catacombs, but stick me in front of a roomful of monkey suits and I just dry up. I need you to impress him at the presentation tonight. *Really* impress him. Or else this

12

whole project is on the line.'

The presentation was to take place in the grand hall of a sixteenth-century *auberge*, built to house the Knights of St John. As she glanced around at the ornate baroque architecture, the trophies, banners and arms, and the long tables littered with the remnants of a sumptuous buffet meal, Venetia wondered how much it had cost Marcus to hire the place for the night – and whether the project could afford it.

Whirling fans purred in high, ornate ceilings and waiters in perfect black and white moved silently among the invited guests, offering glasses of vintage port. Venetia smiled to herself. They were about to discover that there was no such thing as a free meal.

She hoped she looked good. At any rate, she was wearing her best dress – no, it was her *only* really good dress; the blue silk shift she'd worn to visit the casino just outside Nice, on the night she had first set eyes on Esteban . . .

She tried to shake the memory out of her head. Esteban was part of her past, a dangerous excitement that she would do well to forget. But it was as if she had breathed him in and he had become a part of the softly-woven fabric of her soul. It was so easy, too damn easy, to recall the exact sensation of his fingers sliding over her overheated skin, his kisses that started at her lips and moved slowly down the long sweep of her throat until they found the hardening crests of her nipples, pushing eagerly against the fragile, ice-blue silk.

But no. No, she told herself. I don't need you,

Esteban; I thought I did once, but I was mistaken. You have nothing to offer me. Nothing, not ever.

Passing her hand over her brow, she found it moist with a cold sweat. The dress rustled as she moved, its tight sheath opening out into a waterfall of blue silk about her ankles. Glancing to her right, she acknowledged Marcus Hale's nervous, over-formal nod; and Demetrios's suggestive wink. She knew that neither of them had ever seen her dressed like this before – on site, everyone spent all day in shorts or swimsuits – and she wondered eagerly if it turned Marcus on to see her transformed into an English ice-maiden, her breasts full and white against the pale blue silk.

She caught sight of herself in one of the mirrors which lined the sides of the room, and hardly recognised the woman who looked confidently back at her. Her tall, slim figure looked good – no, better than good – in the sophisticated evening dress, her firm, full breasts caressed by the pale blue fabric, nestling in its tight embrace, and her naturally blonde hair coiled up into a loose chignon, with a few tendrils left loose to kiss her cheeks and bare shoulders. Strange how the sight of her reflection struck a chord. The sense of déjà-vu was almost scary. She could almost believe she was back in the South of France, walking into the casino for the first time . . .

'Ladies and gentlemen,' began Marcus. The general chatter subsided a little, but didn't stop. He coughed ineffectually. 'Ladies and gentlemen, thank you for coming here this evening . . .'

The men and women seated in the audience reluctantly put down their drinks and listened. Venetia exchanged a despairing look with one of

14

the expedition's divers. Marcus really was hope-less at this sort of thing. It was no wonder nobody wanted to invest in the project.

'As you know, we are engaged in excavating a number of important sites on the island, including a prehistoric sunken settlement. At present, our work is partly funded by the Maltese Government and the International Council for Undersea Archaeology. However, opportunities have arisen for private investment . . .'

As Marcus droned on, Venetia surveyed the faces dotted around the room. Some, she recognised. There were representatives from the Government, one or two bored-looking newspaper reporters from the *Maltese Times*, a few free-loaders in rented tuxedos. It wasn't difficult to spot who was important and who wasn't. The important ones dressed conservatively, even drably – they were so rich, they didn't need to try.

Quite suddenly, one face caught her eye. The face of a blond, broad-shouldered man in his early forties, blue-eyed and pale-skinned. It was striking rather than handsome, the nose a little crooked, the jaw a little too square. But it was a face which demanded attention. She wondered who he was – a banker perhaps? He had the coolly direct, almost quizzical gaze of a man who wants to know every-thing about everything.

And he was looking straight at her.

Feeling flattered and just a little flirty, Venetia turned away as she heard Marcus speak her name.

'. . . and now Dr Venetia Fellowes, our Opera-tions Director, will explain the project to you in more detail . . .'

Venetia stepped forward, a little nervous now. It

wasn't the prospect of delivering a talk which was making her edgy – it was the blond-haired businessman with the piercing blue eyes. He hadn't stopped looking at her since she'd noticed him in the audience. And even though she wasn't looking at him, she could feel his eyes on her . . .

She began the presentation she had prepared, talking her way easily through the short video-film and slides of the many artefacts which had been raised from the citadel and the temple. It wasn't difficult to talk with real enthusiasm about the project – her work was something she felt passionate about, a real reason for existing.

'And so you see,' she concluded, 'it would be a great tragedy if work were to be halted on these vitally important sites, simply for the lack of adequate funding . . .'

A figure stood up, towering above the other diners. A few heads swivelled in his direction.

'Dr Fellowes.'

Venetia drew in breath as she met his gaze, her mouth suddenly dry. She had known it would be him, even before she turned to look at him.

'Sir?'

'Gabriel Engelhart. I'd like to ask a few questions, if I may.'

'Of course. Ask away.'

'I'd like to have a discussion with you. Outside. If Dr Hale is agreeable.'

Venetia's heart thumped. So this was the man Marcus was so keen for her to impress. He was pretty impressive himself, with his aura of authority, his broad shoulders and sweep of wavy white-blond hair. Not her type though, not her type at all . . .

'Well. I'm not sure, perhaps later. This is rather irregular . . .'

Aware of an interested buzz around her, Venetia glanced at Marcus. He looked pink-faced, sweaty and pathetic.

'Go on,' he mouthed silently. 'Go *on*!'

Excusing herself, Venetia followed Engelhart out of the conference room and into the tiled passageway outside, closing the door behind her.

'I am obliged to you,' said Engelhart, leaning up against the wall, his cream linen suit uncreased even in the sultry evening heat. 'But then, I knew you would agree. You are clearly a woman of some discernment.'

Venetia tried hard not to stare at him. Tonight was strictly business, with lust definitely not on the agenda.

'You wanted to ask me something?' Venetia was at once irritated and intrigued by Engelhart's over-confident manner.

'These excavations . . . why do you consider them so important?'

'They can provide us with a unique insight into one of the great lost civilisations of the ancient world. So little is understood about Maltese prehistory . . .'

'Very possibly,' replied Engelhart coolly. 'But why should I give a damn about the ancient world?'

VIP or not, this man had an arrogance that really got under Venetia's skin.

'I was under the impression that you are an art dealer. Surely you must have a keen interest in the past.'

Engelhart laughed. Venetia had the distinct

impression that he was enjoying himself.

'I am interested in making money.'

'And that is all?'

'Not quite,' Engelhart confessed. 'For instance, I am also interested in you.'

Venetia felt a shiver run through her body. It was impossible to be sure if it was a thrill of excitement or a shudder of repulsion. How could a man both attract and repel in such equal measure?

'I'm not sure I know what you mean,' she said slowly.

'Then allow me to explain.' Engelhart snapped his fingers at a passing waiter and took a glass of wine off his silver tray. He sipped at the chilled liquid. 'It won't take a moment. It is obvious to me that you are an intelligent woman.' He smiled. 'Intelligent as well as beautiful. And you see, Venetia, it wasn't this presentation which brought me to Malta. It was you. I knew I had to have you.'

Venetia took a step back. Was this Engelhart guy on the level, or was he some kind of weirdo out for a cheap thrill?

'Hold on a minute, Mr Engelhart, I've never met you before in my life!'

'True. But I have heard of you. Of your knowledge and your skill – and your courage. Few women would have risked their own lives to save the life of another – particularly not a worthless little airhead like your sister Cassandra . . .'

'I think you should watch what you're saying, Mr Engelhart!'

Engelhart appeared to take not the slightest notice.

'You have what I need, Venetia.'

'Which is?'

'An encyclopaedic knowledge of ancient languages and texts – and a spirit of adventure. I want you to do a job for me.'

'I have a job already.'

'Ah, but for how long? Without funding, I understand that this project will soon be as dead as the sites you've been excavating.'

'Are you trying to blackmail me?'

'Naturally – if that's what it takes.' Engelhart drank the last of his wine and set the glass down on a small marble side-table. 'Let us simply say that if you're prepared to help me, I'm prepared to be more than generous to Dr Hale and his team.'

'What do you want me to do?'

'Tell me, have you ever heard of the *Lore of Madali*?'

An electric buzz of interest raised the hairs on the back of Venetia's neck.

'The *Lore of Madali*? Of course I've heard of it. It's a legend – it doesn't exist.'

History had spoken of an ancient collection of exquisite erotica and esoteric wisdom, but there had never been the slightest evidence that it had ever existed outside the imagination of poets and storytellers.

'Really? You're quite sure?'

'Are you telling me you know where it is?'

'Perhaps. And with your help, Venetia, I am going to possess it.'

Chapter Two

IT WAS A warm, sunny evening, and Venetia was sitting with Marcus Hale outside a waterfront café in Marsaxlokk. In the tiny harbour, brightly-painted *iuzzu* fishing boats bobbed at anchor, their shades of red, blue, green and yellow dazzling in the evening sunshine. On either side of their high prows, carved and painted Eyes of Osiris watched unblinkingly, as they had done for countless centuries.

Marcus pushed away his plate of *fenek-biz-zalza* with a grunt of annoyance. Venetia glanced up.

'What's the matter, Marcus?' she enquired coldly. 'Lost your appetite?'

'Look, Venetia,' he snapped. 'I'm the Director around here, and if I say you're not going, you're not going.'

Venetia and Marcus glared at each other across the table. Venetia took her time and chose her words with relish.

'Marcus, you can be such a bone-headed little shit. Has anybody ever told you that?' That was something she'd been itching to say for ages, and it was worth it just to see the look on his face.

'Really?' replied Marcus icily. 'And have you forgotten that I'm also your employer?'

'True, but for how long?' pointed out Venetia, stabbing her fork into a cube of *gbejna* cheese.

Marcus played with his food, pushing the stewed rabbit around his plate like a sulky child.

'We'll manage without Engelhart's money,' he replied sullenly.

Venetia let out a gasp of exasperation.

'I don't get you, Marcus, really I don't. One minute you're telling me to butter this guy up, so he'll put money into the project; the next, you're practically forbidding me to have anything to do with him.' She looked at him over a forkful of salad. 'I don't suppose you'd be jealous, would you?'

'Don't be bloody stupid,' snapped Marcus, a little too hastily.

'Oh yeah?'

Venetia was beginning to see Marcus Hale in a whole new light. It had never occurred to her to think of him in *that* way before. Marcus was the kind of guy who had sexual relationships with fossils, not people. But now she noticed a look in his eyes. A look that struck a chord. She'd been in and out of enough rocky relationships to recognise the green-eyed monster when she saw it.

'It's the project I'm concerned with,' insisted Marcus. 'Not everyone is obsessed with sex,' he added darkly, no doubt with Demetrios in mind.

'Well, I'm glad to hear that,' replied Venetia breezily. 'Because it's the project I care about, too.

21

And that's why I've decided to accept Gabriel Engelhart's offer.'

'I told you . . .'

'I know what you told me, Marcus, and now it's my turn to tell you. I'm telling you that if Engelhart doesn't bail us out soon, we'll go under. You said so yourself. All he wants me to do is travel with him and help him look for this book he's so keen on. In return, he'll fund the project for another eighteen months.' She got to her feet, pushing away her plate and counting out the money for her share of the bill. 'Oh, and in case you're wondering, I'm going purely for business reasons. Pleasure doesn't come into it.'

Really? thought Marcus gloomily as he watched Venetia's endless, tanned thighs stalking angrily out of the café and off along the waterfront towards the jeep. Could have fooled me.

As luck would have it, Gabriel Engelhart was stepping onto the deck of his yacht at the precise moment when Venetia's jeep pulled up on the quayside at the exclusive resort of Sliema Creek.

He stood there for a moment, just watching her walk along the promenade towards him. She moved like a thoroughbred, her walk at once angry and graceful. Her long, blonde hair was piled in a loose knot on top of her head, baring the long, tanned curve of her neck; and he felt an insane urge to kiss it. She had a good body too, long-legged and spare without being rangy. Her full breasts bobbed free under a low-cut, sleeveless khaki T-shirt.

Jumping over the rail, he landed on the

boardwalk in front of her. She didn't turn a hair, just stood there with that seductive half-smile of hers.

'Miss Fellows. Venetia. How pleasant to see you again. Have you discussed my little proposition with your project director?'

'As a matter of face I have.'

Gabriel's face relaxed and he almost, but not quite, smiled.

'Excellent.'

'What makes you so sure I've decided to accept?'

'First, you're no fool. Second, you look angry. That leads me to believe you've just told Dr Hale something he didn't want to hear.'

'You think you know everything, don't you?'

She was beginning to wonder if she'd made the wrong decision after all. Gabriel Engelhart was such an opinionated pig of a man. But it was too late to get cold feet now. Gabriel stroked his hand down her bare shoulder.

'I know you, Venetia.'

She tried to step away, escaping his touch, but their eyes met and suddenly she felt her whole body responding to him; aroused, sensual, seductively willing. His eyes seemed both to caress and to command, taking away all her determination to keep her distance.

'I know you, Venetia; but I intend to know you much better.'

Unseen by Gabriel and Venetia, the shadowy figure of a man was watching from the quayside. As Gabriel slid his arm around Venetia's waist and drew her into a kiss, the man turned and walked quickly away, into the first rays of the sunset.

The yacht *Deliverance III* was far bigger and more luxurious than anything Venetia had ever seen before.

The nearest she had come to it was two years previously, when she had spent time in the South of France, tracking down her twin sister, Cassie. It had been there that she had her first taste of luxury villas, casinos and the champagne life-style; of sophisticated men like Bastien LeRocq . . . and Esteban.

Out here on the sunlit sea, heading out across the Mediterranean towards North Africa, Esteban seemed no more than a wild dream, a fantasy capable of existing only in darkness and shadow. Perhaps it had never existed. Perhaps Esteban himself was nothing more than the creation of her own deepest, darkest, most secret desires. And now she had left that wild, dark fantasy far behind. She was free of him now – or was she? She could never be quite free of the memory of him, or the terrible, tortured passion he had made her feel.

Standing on deck, looking out over the breathtaking blue of the sea, she allowed herself to remember what had passed between them. Esteban, the dark-haired gambler, her vampire lover, had won the price of her life and then, inexplicably, set her free. But there were some things you could never be quite free of. How could she ever forget the thrill of his tongue, lapping at the swollen pink pearl of her clitoris; the exquisite, savage danger of their coupling?

The hot sun caressed her bare shoulders. She

24

took the pins from her hair and let it fall in a glossy cascade down her back. It felt silky, sensual, like a lover's hand smoothing her bare flesh.

A voice behind her woke her from her reverie.

'Why don't you take it off?'

She wheeled round. Gabriel Engelhart was standing behind her, naked but for the fluffy white bathtowel tied around his waist. In the noonday sun, his pale skin seemed creamy rather than pallid; the smooth perfection of Italian marble.

'Why don't you take off your shirt?' he repeated. 'You'd be much cooler.'

She shook her head, at once very tempted and vaguely embarrassed. It still seemed incredible that she should have agreed to go on this wild goose-chase with a complete stranger. Let alone one who could make her feel lust and loathing in equal measure.

'When will we arrive?' she asked him.

Engelhart glanced at his watch.

'We should reach Tunis in about twelve hours. I have been given the name of a contact there, a man called Yusuf.' He came up behind her. He did not touch her, but Venetia found herself wishing that he would.

'And he knows where to find the book?'

'Perhaps. If not, he will know where we should look. I am told that he, like you, is knowledgeable about ancient texts.' He paused, breathing in the fresh flower-scent of Venetia's body. 'I hear he also has an eye for a pretty Englishwoman. You will doubtless be able to obtain far more information from him than I could.'

'You really believe the *Lore of Madali* exists, don't you?'

'And you don't?'

She shrugged.

'I'm a scientist. I'll believe it when I see it.'

'It is said to be very beautiful, you know. Think of it: hundreds of exquisite erotic miniatures, and all the sexual wisdom of the ancient world. Wouldn't you like to know the secrets of perpetual pleasure? I know I would.'

Venetia's mouth was dry. She could feel Gabriel very close behind her, almost but not quite touching, his breath hot on the nape of her neck.

'I suppose anyone would.'

She pretended to gaze out over the sea, but all her thoughts were concentrated on Gabriel, her body yearning for some soft caress, some touch that might satisfy the hunger within her.

His hand stroked her shoulder and she started, her whole body shuddering at the touch.

'You are very tense, Venetia. You should try to relax more.'

His strong fingers began kneading her shoulders through her filmy cotton shirt, and she leant back, offering herself to the gesture. It felt good. Too good to resist for long, and Venetia had been too long without physical comfort. How long was it since she had enjoyed Demetrios's caresses? Only two days and nights, and yet her body was strung tight as a wire, singing in the wind.

'Mmm.' Her enjoyment escaped in a soft sigh from her parted lips.

'So very tense. All your muscles are knotted. Here, let me ease them for you. Just relax.'

Gabriel's fingers were strong and supple. As

26

they kneaded her shoulders, Venetia yielded to the seductive strength, the smooth insistence of the caress. And it *was* a caress, there could be no doubt of that. Somewhere at the back of her mind, Venetia wondered idly how she could feel so suddenly and so strongly attracted to this man – this self-opinionated man who wasn't even her type. A man who, on their first meeting, had seemed to undress her with his eyes . . .

She could hear his breathing, soft and low. Felt him bend closer over her, caught her breath as his lips brushed lightly across the back of her neck.

'Take it off, Venetia. Who's to see?'

He's right, thought Venetia, caught in a happy haze of lazy sensuality. Who's to see? And quickly unbuttoning her Indian cotton shirt, she peeled it off and let it fall to the deck.

She was bare to the waist now, her lightly-tanned breasts a testament to the amount of time she had spent working naked on the isolated Maltese beaches.

'You have a remarkable body, Venetia,' breathed Gabriel. She looked over her shoulder at him, but he shook his head. 'No, don't turn round. Stay where you are. Let me make you feel good.'

Gabriel slid his hands round Venetia's waist. At first he made no attempt to caress her, but he pressed his body against hers, his bare chest rubbing against the top of her back, the fine wire of flaxen hairs tickling her skin. She felt his right hand move behind her, followed by the soft slithering of the bathtowel as he unfastened it and let it fall.

'Quite remarkable,' he repeated, and held her

more tightly against him. Now she could feel the strength of his desire. His penis was hardening, lengthening; nuzzling into the small of her back, its moistening tip leaving a lick of wetness on her golden skin.

'Please, Gabriel, I don't think . . .' she began. But it was all show. She and he both knew what they wanted. It was just a matter of time before the last, small resistance melted away.

'You must be uncomfortable in those shorts. Here, let me help you out of them.'

Venetia let out a giggle of protest, but Gabriel gently lifted her protesting hand away from the waistband of her shorts. His fingers were swift and adept, flicking open the fastening with a light click. Then the zipper yielded, sliding slowly down with a soft sigh of release.

'There, isn't that better? Doesn't that feel good?'

He eased down her shorts and, still facing away from him, she stepped out of them. Underneath she was wearing thin white cotton briefs, moist and semi-transparent with sweat. Gabriel's appreciative fingertip traced the dark curve marking the deep valley between her buttocks.

'You shouldn't . . . we shouldn't . . .' Venetia felt utterly stupid. Here she was, protesting like some timorous virgin, and all the time her shameless body was betraying her, her nipples hard as carved wood, her outer labia plump and swollen, her panties wet and fragrant with her need. 'You know we shouldn't . . .'

'Why not, Venetia? You're surely not afraid of pleasure?'

'It's not that. It's just . . . this is too soon . . .'

This time, Gabriel kissed her with real insistence, his lips pressing hard again and again, along the line of her back, her shoulder-blade, the soaring upward sweep of her neck. For a split second, she almost imagined she was with Esteban again, thrilling to the exquisite danger of his kiss, the fear and the pleasure so inextricably mingled.

'There's really nothing to fear, Venetia.'

'W-what makes you think I'm afraid?'

'You're shaking. Shaking all over, I can feel it.'

Gabriel's hands slid abruptly upward, smoothing over her ribcage until they met the firm, warm overhang of her breasts.

'Even your breasts are trembling. Quivering all over. It makes me want to hold them and keep them safe.'

Venetia let out a low groan of excitement as his fingers climbed higher, so so slowly, grazing the flesh with the utmost tenderness, teasing and arousing with each butterfly touch.

'Gabriel, please . . .'

Was she asking him to free her from his embrace, or to go on and on and on and never stop? She didn't want to confess the truth, even to herself. But as his fingertips closed about her breasts, forming the sweetest, softest cage of pleasure, she pressed herself more tightly into this delicious captivity.

Gabriel purred with satisfaction. Venetia was even more sensual than he had anticipated. She made his cock rear like a stallion's, made the blood pump round his body in an exhilaration of lust. He squeezed and palpated Venetia's breasts, skilfully catching the nipples between his fingers

29

and pinching them tightly. Her gasps of excitement intensified his pleasure, made him long to be inside her.

'Do you want me?' he breathed into her ear.

Venetia let out a low answering sob, pushing out her backside so that it rubbed against the erect shaft of Gabriel's penis. Now it was his turn to gasp in excitement as the wet cotton fabric slid roughly over his exposed glans, almost provoking him to a climax.

'I want you, Venetia. I've wanted you ever since we met.' Or even longer, he thought to himself with satisfaction. Even the idea of Venetia Fellowes had seemed erotic to him, and the reality was so very much more appealing.

His fingers slid down and under the sides of Venetia's white briefs.

'You don't need these any more, do you?'

Taking his hands from her thighs, Venetia turned slowly round until she was looking him full in the face. She was smiling, breathing a little heavily.

'I can undress myself,' she murmured. 'Watch me.'

She rolled down her panties with infinite slowness, savouring the look of torment on Gabriel's face. She knew that he was a man who couldn't bear not to be in control; and here he was, forced to watch as she danced before him, slowly stripping away the last veil of her modesty.

Her honeygold pubic curls emerged, crisp and glossy in the Mediterranean sun; neatly clipped into a springy tuft which begged to be kissed.

'Venetia, you little witch, I have to have you.'

Venetia swung back her hair, and the silky curtain flew out behind her in the sea-wind. She felt strong, invulnerable.

'Then take me. Kiss me. Why don't you kiss me?'

For a moment Venetia wondered if she had made the wrong move, misjudged the game. Maybe Engelhart only liked women who were willing to play the sweet submissive. Then Gabriel's spellbound face relaxed into a grin, and he threw back his head and laughed.

'You're a shameless slut, Venetia Fellowes.'

'And you're complaining?'

'Not in the least. But of course, if you play the slut, you have to take the consequences . . .'

He gathered her up in his arms, so suddenly that she had no time to resist, even for a second. The next thing she knew, Gabriel had balanced her on the ship's rail, so that she was leaning back, half-in and half-out of the yacht.

'Gabriel . . . what the hell are you doing?' she squealed, half-terrified and half-exhilarated by his recklessness.

'I'm taking you. You wanted me to, don't you remember?'

His hands cupped her buttocks as he stood between her outspread thighs. Venetia stretched out her hands and grasped the rail on either side, hardly daring to open her eyes, caught as she was between the blazing summer sky and the fathomless glitter of the sea below.

'If you drop me, Gabriel Engelhart . . .'

'You'll just have to trust me not to, won't you?'

Trust . . . how could she trust this stranger, this mad adventurer who had simply strolled into her

31

life and taken it over? And yet the knowledge of the very great risk she was taking only served to add extra spice to this crazy moment.

Gabriel's body was hot and hard between her thighs. She could not see him, only feel the great dark shadow he cast across her body, moving between her and the sun.

Still holding on to her with his left hand, he used his right to explore his prey.

'Such silky thighs you have, Venetia. Do you wax your thighs? I'd love to pour wine all over that creamy skin and lick it off, every drop. What do you say, shall we do that?'

Venetia tried hard not to wriggle as he stroked her inner thighs, half-caressing, half-tickling.

'Oh – oh Gabriel, don't, I'll fall . . .'

'Don't you trust me not to let you fall? Don't you? I thought you said you weren't afraid of anything.'

For a moment, he let go of her with both hands and she was balancing precariously on the narrow wooden rail, poised only seconds away from the rushing water beneath. She knew he was taunting her, and swore to herself that he would not win. By some massive effort of will, she managed not to cry out, though her heart was thumping with fear.

Tightening her thighs about Gabriel's, she forced the tremor from her voice.

'Fuck me. I want to be fucked.'

He growled with pleasure, seizing hold of her backside with one hand whilst the other explored the moist and tender heart of her sex, his fingertip drawing patterns in the sweet, wet ooze which glistened on the coral-pink folds of her inner labia.

Venetia's whole body was shaking, pulsing to

the desperate throb of her swollen clitoris. And all the time, Gabriel was torturing her with that sultry, mocking voice.

'What have we here? A pink rosebud? A juicy pink rosebud. And what's this at the very centre? It's a shiny little pearl. Let me feel how hard it is . . .'

The touch of his fingertip on her exposed clitoris was the briefest, the lightest contact imaginable, but it felt as though a huge electric shock were being passed through her body. This time she couldn't suppress the cry, which tore from her from between her parted lips.

'Bastard . . . bastard, don't do this to me!'

'But it's what you've always wanted, isn't it? The chance to live dangerously?'

Suddenly, quite without warning, he slid the tip of his penis into the welcoming entrance to her womanhood. She shuddered, writhed, moaned aloud in the torment of her own shameless lust. It was no use playing the blushing virgin now, her secret was out. She wanted this every bit as much as Gabriel did. And her hips thrust forward, inviting him deeper into the wetness of her sex.

With a second thrust he was inside her, up to the hilt. She felt the weight of his testes, full and heavy, resting in the deep valley of her sex; and the fat hardness of his shaft, the blissful, unending length of his penis as it drove into her, accepting the gift of her sexual need.

Their bodies drove together, slick and slippery with sweat. A sweet, thick ooze of juice trickled from Venetia's sex, anointing her lover's manhood, so that it glistened like smooth, polished glass.

Head hanging down and her long curtain of hair

swinging beneath her, Venetia glimpsed the white wake surging and foaming around the boat's hull. It felt as though the wild, churning waters were inside her, bubbling and fizzing in her belly. With each new thrust, Gabriel seemed deeper inside her, and his cock awoke a new world of sensations, sparkling and irresistible.

She heard laughter; her own. This reckless, foolish pleasure was carrying her beyond herself and into a realm where nothing mattered but the moment.

Tightening her thighs about Gabriel's waist, she felt his fingers clutching hard at her buttocks. His grip was tight, muscular, determined; the unforgiving caress of a man who knows what he wants – and what his lover wants also. She writhed instinctively as his pelvis ground against hers, provoking ripples of ecstasy as he brushed against the hard nubbin of her clitoris. But Gabriel did not loosen his grip. On the contrary, his fingers clenched more tightly around the soft, firm flesh of her buttocks, drawing them further apart, opening up the secret world within.

'Oh. Oh. Oh.' Her little cries escaped in little outrushes of breath, set to the rhythm of Gabriel's eager thrusts.

'Take it. Take it,' he grunted, utterly crazy for the hot, wet paradise of Venetia's sex. He had judged her to be a profoundly sensual woman, but had hardly expected her haven to be so welcoming and so deliciously tight.

'No . . . no more. I can't . . .' moaned Venetia. She felt stretched beyond capacity, her whole body filled up with the swollen hardness of Gabriel's dick. 'I really can't . . .' But she wanted more. She craved more and more and more; for each movement, each caress, brought her nearer to the top of the blissful rollercoaster . . .

She had thought there could be no more, but Gabriel had hardly begun. Releasing his grip slightly, he allowed his fingers to slide deeper into the amber furrow between Venetia's buttocks.

'Gabriel, no! Don't do that, I don't want you to . . .'

It was Gabriel who was laughing now; mocking her pretended modesty.

'My beautiful liar, are you telling me no man has ever touched you *here*?'

His fingertip slid, very lightly, along the sensitive membrane, lingering fleetingly on the tight-closed rosebud of her anus. Venetia's whole body seemed to contract in upon itself, the blossom as her anus trembled and dilated at her lover's touch. She squealed, half in outrage, half in pleasure.

'Don't fight me,' breathed Gabriel, withdrawing his penis and tantalising her aching sex, only to slide it back into her with teasing, exhilarating slowness. 'Let it happen. You know it's what you want. *I* know it's what you want.'

Venetia's heart was pounding, her head dizzy and spinning from the rush of blood to her brain. She felt dreamy and phantasmagorical, a make-believe woman in a fantastic world, weightless and unreal. Only the pleasure existed, and that was hot, and strong, and tyrannical in its relentless power.

'Do it,' she murmured. 'Do it to me.'

Gabriel needed no further persuasion. Already

his fingertip was teasing the amber rose, gently tickling and stroking the quivering petals, persuading them, little by little, to open and let him in.

When his finger slid into her behind, she shivered with a silent, private ecstasy. The double torment of his penis and his finger, toiling together inside her, left her helpless to do anything but simply allow herself to be carried on the wild wave of pleasure.

'Come for me. I want you to come. And then I want you to come again and again.'

Gabriel's voice half-coaxed, half-commanded. Something at the back of Venetia's mind wanted to resist this sensual arrogance, this man who seemed to know so much about her, but the power of pleasure was far too great. And when he pushed himself that last, blissful millimetre into the hot depths of her, her clitoris sang for joy. Its hard stalk rubbed brutally against Gabriel's pubic bone. The sensation was not sweet or gentle; it was an electric stab which transformed itself instantly into the first, unbelievably wonderful spasm of climax.

As her body relaxed into the long, delicate, dying waves of orgasm, Venetia felt Gabriel ejaculate. He remained inside her for many long moments, the only sounds around them the rhythm of their breathing and the distant thunder of the sea.

It was evening when *Deliverance III* sailed into Tunis harbour. The port was almost deserted as darkness fell; but there was one who watched, unseen, from the shadows. A creature of darkness and silence.

Gabriel Engelhart turned and called down to Venetia.

'Come up here. We're almost there.'

Slipping on a loose shirt over her bikini, Venetia climbed up the steps from the cabin and joined Gabriel on deck. She stood close to him but not touching; not feeling any urge to do any of the things that lovers do, like slipping her arm through his. It was as though they both sensed that their intimacy was not of that kind. Oddly, Venetia felt more distant from him than she had done before they had had sex.

The harbour lights glittered before them, lighting up the velvety sky.

'What will we do when we arrive?' asked Venetia.

'Tonight we will stay at a house I have in the town. Tomorrow, we will seek out Yusuf.'

'Who is he, this Yusuf?'

Gabriel shrugged.

'I know little of him, except that he is an art dealer, a bit of a rogue. But my information tells me that he will help us – if the price is right.'

They docked in the marina and Gabriel helped Venetia onto the quayside. Together they walked towards the *poste de douane*, where a group of uniformed customs officers with guns stood lounging about, smoking.

'*Passeports, m'sieur dame,*' grunted one of the *douaniers*, thrusting out a massive paw of a hand. Gabriel handed his over and it was handed back after a cursory glance. But Venetia's was passed from hand to hand.

'Is there a problem?' enquired Venetia, sud-

37

denly uneasy. She had seen the expressions on the men's faces, the knowing smiles as they passed around the passport. '*Est-ce qu'il y a un problème?*'

'*Peut-être*,' replied the senior customs officer. His hand lingered on Venetia's arm and she froze to the spot. His fingers brushed the side of her breast as he looked her up and down. '*Venez avec moi*. You must come with us for . . .' He winked. 'Questioning.'

Venetia felt panic rising inside her.

'Why? What have I done?'

A hand took her by the elbow.

'Come with us. You must come with us.'

But they had not reckoned with Gabriel Engelhart.

'Leave her alone. *Laissez! Vous m'entendez?*'

The customs officer wheeled round to look at Gabriel.

'*Quoi?*'

'I said, leave her alone.' Gabriel reached into his pocket, took out some sort of identity card and flashed it briefly. 'Unless, of course, you would like to explain this to the Chief of Police.'

Venetia was amazed by the transformation. Leers became respectful smiles, and the hand was removed from her arm as swiftly as it had grabbed hold of her.

'Everything is in order, *madame*. I hope you have an enjoyable stay.'

Pocketing her passport, Venetia followed Gabriel out of the customs house, intrigued.

'How did you do that?' she asked.

'I make it my business to know useful people.'

'Evidently.' She caught up with him. 'Thanks, anyway.'

He inclined his head towards her.

'It is of no consequence. Besides, I have to protect my investment. Tomorrow you begin work on making me my next million.'

Chapter Three

GABRIEL'S HOUSE WAS tucked away in a side-street, its façade modest and peeling, in the middle of a row of once-grand, now run-down colonial houses. Venetia blinked in disbelief.

'We are in the district of the *foundouks*,' explained Gabriel as the car manoeuvred awkwardly along the rutted road. 'These buildings were once foreign embassies, but they are now used as *oukala*, apartments for poor people.' He grinned as he added, 'The red light district begins just down there, at the end of *rue Zarkoun*.'

Gabriel opened the car door and Venetia stepped out into the street, conscious even at this late hour that eyes were watching her from all sides, a few shabby children staring wide-eyed at her from crumbling doorways.

'This is it – your house?'

Gabriel gave a throaty chuckle.

'Not quite what you expected?'

'Well . . . I mean – why *here*?'

'The great advantage of this district is that it is very secluded, very discreet. Rich tourists do not come here, they are too afraid. Come inside. I think you will be surprised.'

Gabriel's chauffeur got out and knocked on the front door. A few seconds later a grille slid open. A face peered out, dark-eyed and swarthy.

'Master!'

'Open up, Ismail. We have a guest tonight.'

The heavy door swung open, to reveal a middle-aged Arab in traditional white robes, standing in a dusty inner courtyard. Hands pressed together, he executed a small, respectful salaam.

'Ismail, this is Miss Fellowes.'

'Madame.' The dark eyes lingered, then were lowered, rather reluctantly, thought Venetia. She could feel those eyes boring into her, even after he had looked away.

'You may take our luggage up to the Balcony Room.'

'At once, master.'

Ismail led the way, Venetia following Gabriel across the dusty courtyard towards a second door, this one guarded by a very beautiful gilded gate. Once on the other side of the door, Venetia let out a gasp of astonishment.

'I told you you would be surprised,' commented Gabriel. 'You really must try to believe what I tell you.'

They were standing in a vast circular entrance hall, lined with twisted pillars of gilded marble. In the centre was a sunken pond, filled with shimmering gold and silver fish; and above arched a high domed ceiling, painted dark blue and decorated with intricate, many-coloured filigree patterns in the Islamic style.

41

'It's incredible!' exclaimed Venetia. So, she thought to herself, Gabriel Engelhart must be even wealthier than I thought.

'I like all my villas to be decorated in the local style,' explained Gabriel airily.

'How many do you have?'

'Oh, six – no, seven. I was forgetting the new place I'm having built in the Hollywood Hills.'

Venetia shook her head in disbelief.

'It doesn't sound as if you need the *Lore of Madali*.'

'Oh, I don't. Not for the money.' Gabriel took a stray strand of Venetia's hair, kissed it and stroked it down. 'But I *desire* it. And whatever I desire, I simply must have.' His hand rested lightly on the back of Venetia's neck. 'I have sought it for years, and soon it will be mine.'

'If we ever find it.'

'We will – no, *you* will find it for me. And when I have enjoyed owning it for a while, I shall enjoy selling it on for a very large sum of money. Now, if you are ready, we shall go to our rooms and Ismail shall serve us dinner.'

The roof garden of Gabriel's villa was illuminated by soft, rose-pink lights hidden among the tangle of greenery.

Vines twined overhead, heavy trusses of juicy fruit fragrant and glossy in the soft light. Peach, nectarine and citrus trees gave off a declicate, tangy scent which mingled with the heavier perfumes of roses, mimosa and night-scented jasmine.

Ismail arrived to serve dessert: a silver salver of sticky-sweet halva, honey-soaked *makroudh*, stuffed dates, and a pot of *té akhdar* – green tea with mint, sprinkled with pine nuts and almonds.

'All is as you wish it, master?'

'It is perfectly satisfactory. You may leave us now.'

Ismail made an obsequious bow and took his leave. Venetia felt a surge of relief. She had already decided that she did not like Gabriel's taste in servants.

Gabriel poured the mint tea into two small enamelled cups.

'Ismail is a devoted servant,' he told Venetia, his eyes caressing her, never leaving her face. 'He would quite happily die for me. Absolute loyalty is a quality I prize highly.'

'I'm . . . sure.'

'But you find him a little too . . . attentive?' Gariel searched her face.

'Perhaps.' She didn't add that, frankly, Ismail gave her the creeps, with his look of a hungry mongrel dog.

'Among his other accomplishments, Ismail is a very fine judge of women.' Gabriel leaned closer. 'Before he came to me, he was a procurer.'

'A what?'

'A procurer of beautiful girls for harems and houses of pleasure. He still has an eye for a fine-looking European woman like you. He is probably wondering what price I am intending to ask for you . . .'

The colour drained from Venetia's face. 'I hope this is some kind of joke, because if it isn't I think I'd better leave . . .'

Gabriel laid his hand on her arm. 'I am sorry, I have no desire to alarm you. You are quite safe

43

here.' Taking her hand, he pressed it to his lips. They felt feverish and hot against her chilled flesh. 'You are perfectly free – free to stay or to go, just as you choose. Although I should remind you that you are here to help your colleagues in Malta. Without my very generous contribution . . .'

Venetia sat down and sipped her coffee. 'I don't know how to take you. I can't figure you out at all.'

'You think of me as an enigma? Really, I am flattered.'

'You're making fun of me.'

'Now, would I do that?'

She looked up at him. 'Almost certainly. It seems to me that you do just about any damn thing you feel like doing.'

Gabriel reached out and picked up a remote handset. A second later, soft Eastern music began playing, its rhythms complex and deeply sensual.

'You enjoy Syrian music, Venetia?'

'As a matter of fact I do. It's so . . . haunting. I spent time in Syria when I was an undergraduate, working on a dig.'

'I know. That is one of the reasons I chose you. You see, I have certain information . . . a rumour that what we seek has been taken to Eastern Syria.' Gabriel got up and slid onto the pile of cushions next to Venetia. 'But for now, all I want is to know more about you.'

A slight breeze ruffled the light, gauzy hangings and the lights seemed to flicker. Glancing up, Venetia could have sworn that, for a few brief seconds, shadows chased each other across the surface of the moon.

Gabriel's hand released the pins from Venetia's

hair and as it tumbled down her back he smoothed it down, as though he were stroking a cat. Venetia responded with a soft murmur of appreciation. This man truly was an enigma to her – one moment so arrogant and opinionated, the next, softly caressing.

'There's nothing to know about me. I'm just . . . ordinary.'

'Oh no, Venetia. Not ordinary at all; you must cure yourself of this false modesty. You are the most extraordinary woman I know. Extraordinarily attractive, certainly; but more than that. You see, I sensed the need within you the moment I first saw you.'

'The need? What need?'

'The need for pleasure. You are an animal, Venetia; a sensual animal. You need to use your body for pleasure, it is as natural an exercise for you as breathing. I'm right, aren't I?'

He stroked his hand down the inside of her arm and she trembled slightly at the unexpected intensity of sensation.

'Look, Gabriel . . . what happened on the boat . . .'

'You're not telling me that you regret it?'

'No, not exactly . . . but . . .'

'But nothing. Let go, Venetia, stop feeling guilty for once in your life. Let me liberate all this need inside you. It will be so easy.'

He was right next to her, his hand hot against her skin, the imprint of his caress unforgettable and tingling on her bare arm. Gently he took her in his arms and kissed her, his lips coaxing hers to respond. And she could not resist, for excitement was trembling through her whole body already.

As he drew away, he left her panting, her lips glistening with wetness.

'You really think you're God, don't you, Gabriel Engelhart?'

'Tonight, I'm whatever you want me to be.'

'Oh yes?' She returned his gaze defiantly, calling his bluff. 'And if I wanted you to be my helpless sex-slave?'

He chuckled. 'Ah, but you don't, do you? That's exactly what you don't want me to be. A woman like you needs to be possessed . . .'

Their lips met again, and this time, she returned the passion of Gabriel's kiss. She wanted to tell him to go to hell, but her body was whispering to her of pleasure, treacherously aching for more and still more. Parting her lips, she allowed her tongue to slide into his mouth, the taste of mint tea and sweetness mingling as they kissed.

He pushed her down gently onto the heap of embroidered cushions, and she slipped down willingly, letting him think he had the measure of her. He lay half-on, half-beside her, his thigh sliding over hers as his hands roamed over her breasts. He unfastened the top button of her shirt, then the second, revealing the pink push-up bra underneath, and the creamy swell of her cleavage.

It would have been the easiest thing in the world just to let Gabriel do whatever he wanted with her. But Venetia wanted more.

'Want me?' she murmured as he unfastened her shirt and pushed it free of her breasts.

'You know I do.'

'You promised to be whatever I want you to be.'

'Anything.'

Supple as a cat, she rolled sideways, so that

Gabriel was underneath and she was half on top of him, her thigh across his legs. Propping herself up on one elbow, she gazed down at him, her lips pouting into a self-satisfied smile. Gabriel gazed back at her, half-puzzled and half-appreciative.

'You're full of surprises tonight, my English cat,' he grinned.

'It's high time you felt my claws.'

Venetia could hardly believe she was talking like this to Gabriel Engelhart, the man Marcus Hale had marked down as the saviour of the Maltese project. The man she was supposed to be *working* for, for goodness sake. On the other hand, she could hardly believe that she had slipped so easily into a red-hot liaison with a man she knew nothing about and hardly even liked. Perhaps it was the summer sun, the wine, the warm North African night, but right here and now it felt like exactly the right thing to do.

Her fingers ran over Gabriel's face, down his cheek, the side of his neck and onto his chest; scoring the flesh lightly with her varnished nails. Then she bent to kiss the flesh she had martyred, moistening the skin with cooling saliva, darting a myriad tiny kisses from brow to the nape of Gabriel's neck. As she kissed him, her fingers worked at the buttons of his silk shirt, opening it like the wrapping on a gift, peeling it back to expose the smooth skin beneath.

'You sexy bitch,' groaned Gabriel as she ran her nails up and down his belly and chest. He was well-muscled, firm; his skin smooth and hairless, defining the contours of his powerful body. 'How do you know just what to do to drive me mad?'

Her unspoken reply was to reach down his

belly until her fingers met the buckle of his belt. She had no need of words to show him how she could give him pleasure. She slipped the buckle and slid it away from his body. The leather felt supple and smooth in her hand.

'I could tie your wrists with this,' she teased.

'You wouldn't though.' He looked at her quizzically, as though seeing her afresh. 'You're not that kind of girl.'

'Oh, but I would. And I am. What's more, you promised you'd be whatever I wanted you to be.'

'For tonight.'

'For tonight.' Venetia looked at him from under the sweep of her eyelashes. 'Tomorrow night, who knows . . .?'

Gabriel decided that he would play her at this game; it was a novelty to him – and he liked his women to provide him with a few surprises. This one was more adventurous and exciting than he had imagined. And he had already found her exceptionally stimulating, with her pretty, submissive face and her sensual ways.

He reached his wrists up above his head, and Venetia looped the belt around them several times, tying them comfortably, but firmly enough to hold them fast.

'Now you're mine,' she smiled. And lowering herself onto him, she kissed, licked and bit into the sweat-seasoned flesh of his nipples.

'Bitch! You outrageous bitch . . .' Gabriel's voice was more full of admiration than outrage.

He twisted and turned and wriggled, but could not escape the tyrannical pleasure of her savage little kisses. She was astride his waist, and he could feel the heat of her, soaking into him through her panties. She felt hot and moist, and he could smell her sweetness, the seductive odour which signalled her readiness for him.

And he was so, so ready for her. His manhood ached with the need of her, pushing its swollen head against the inside of his shorts. He moved his pelvis under her, pushing himself against her, thrusting between her legs; but still she went on sucking and biting his nipples, her free hand raking nail-tips down over his bare flesh. It was hell; or it was heaven? All he knew for sure was that he didn't want it to stop.

At last Venetia tired of her game, and knelt up. Her mouth was wet with her own saliva and Gabriel's sweat.

'Your nipples have gone all hard.' She stroked the flat of her hands over them, and Gabriel's body started at the exquisiteness of her touch.

'And yours?' Gabriel's sapphire-blue eyes demanded an answer. 'Are your nipples hard for me? Wouldn't you like me to suck and bite them?'

'First, I want to see you naked,' replied Venetia, running the tip of her tongue over her lips, discovering a new and insatiable thirst.

She unbuttoned Gabriel's trousers. There was no zip, just a line of beautiful mother-of-pearl buttons; old-fashioned and very, very classy. This man intrigued her. Unconventional, arrogant, exuberantly confident, he was completely different from any other lover she had ever had.

Except perhaps Esteban . . .

Banishing the fleeting memory from her thoughts, she turned attention to Gabriel's fly-buttons. There were altogether too many of them, and they were just too darn fiddly. The solution was simple.

Bending over him, she set about biting off the buttons, one by one. She felt him shiver at her touch, breathed in the acrid, spicy odour of his manhood, which still bore all the scents of their first coupling. She longed to take it into her mouth, to devour it, to drink down its elixir; but tonight she wanted to be in control. She wanted to savour these moments of unbridled power.

'Lift up your backside,' she told him. He saw no reason not to obey, and she slid down first his trousers, then his silk boxer shorts.

His penis was just a little over average length, but thick and bulbous at the tip. It reared up above large and heavy testes, the right slightly larger and lower than the left; hard and juicy within its taut seed-pod.

'Take it in your mouth,' urged Gabriel, his voice soft and mellifluous, almost hypnotic. It was a tempting prospect.

'Later.'

'I want you.'

'I know. And I'm going to make you want me more.'

Now he was naked before her, delicious in his vulnerability. Who would have thought that Gabriel Engelhart would ever allow himself to look vulnerable? It seemed only fair to even up the score.

'What to see some more, Gabriel?'

He did not answer, but he was devouring her with his eyes. Venetia slipped the shirt from her shoulders and reached round to unfasten her bra. As the catch yielded, the cups sprang away from her breasts, and she slipped the bra off, dropping it onto the ground. Gabriel motioned that he wanted to get up, to touch her, for her to untie him, but she shook her head.

'You promised, remember? Anything I want you to be. And what I want you to be is my very obedient slave.' She laughed. 'Tonight, you can be my Ismail. Lie still now, don't you dare move.'

Two lengths of scarlet silk cord held back the curtains of the canopied pergola. They were perfect for what Venetia had in mind. Swiftly she untied them.

Gabriel watched, guessing what she intended.

'You're not going to try and tie me up with those?'

'Why shouldn't I?' She smiled as she echoed Gabriel's own words. 'You know it's what you want . . .'

He made only a token resistance as Venetia slipped the red cord about his ankles and attached them to the base of the curtained pergola.

'Perfect.'

She knelt back on her haunches to appreciate the full effect of her handiwork.

'So what are you going to do to me now that you have me at your mercy?' he demanded with ironic humour.

'I'm going to take my revenge.'

'Revenge! What's that supposed to mean?'

'It means I'm going to make you feel like you made me feel this morning, when you drove me crazy. It means I'm going to take you right to the edge and keep you there until you beg for mercy.'

'I want you, Venetia.'

His voice, low and soft, awoke a trickle of

pleasure-juice between her pussy-lips, soaking into her already-wet briefs.

'I know you do.'

'I want to fuck you. Do you understand that? I want you *now*.'

'And you shall. When I've had my fun.'

'You need me. I'm the only one who really knows how to give you pleasure. Remember – on the boat . . .'

'I remember.' She laughed, deep and warm and confident. 'But I don't need a man to give me pleasure. I can do that myself.'

Standing up, she slipped her briefs down over her backside, down her hips, her thighs; the moist fabric caressing the sunkissed skin. She watched Gabriel's face, enjoying the look that passed across it as her clipped blonde triangle came into view. It wasn't as if he hadn't seen it all before, but here, now, he wanted so much to kiss and touch and fuck it, simply because it was forbidden.

She stood right over him, her thighs parted, her plump sex-lips parted in a kiss of welcome. The rose-pink light filtered through the vine-leaves, the scent of mimosa and jasmine mingling with the sweet spiciness of her blossoming sex.

'Let me show you what you're missing.' With her fingers, she opened up the soft, dewy-fresh petals of her womanhood, unveiling the secret inner beauty: the glistening well of honeydew, constantly renewed from some hidden spring; the plump, hardened stalk of her clitoris, pushing insolently out from underneath its flesh cowl. 'Do you like what you see?'

'You're a wicked, beautiful slut and I want you right now.'

Gabriel pulled hard against the straps which bound him, and almost succeeded in hauling himself into a sitting position. But Venetia stretched out her right foot – still clad in high-heeled, strappy evening shoes – and pushed him gently but firmly down again.

'You're mine for tonight. I'll tell you when you can have what you want. Now, why don't I show you what I do when I don't have a man around?'

Glancing to her left, she saw a small onyx-topped table inlaid with gold and silver flowers. On top stood many-branched candelabra, shaped like gnarled trees whose bodies took the form of beautiful men and women. Venetia took one of the unlit, red candles and ran her fingers over it. She smiled.

'It's not as big as you, of course, but I think we can still have a little fun.'

Excitement was fizzing in her veins now, the adrenaline of sexual arousal making her half-crazy. Several glasses of excellent champagne had made her head swim, and she felt liberated from the clear-headed, intellectual, ever-so-slightly boring young woman whose life revolved around tomb inscriptions and ancient texts. In the morning she might feel embarrassed about this, even frightened by her own audacity; but the wine and the exotic surroundings and the presence of this attractive, arrogant man made her feel reckless and free.

She heard Gabriel gasp as she parted her outer labia with the fingers of her left hand, and with her right rubbed the rounded end of the candle over the slippery inner folds.

'Mmm, feels good,' she purred. 'Could you

make me feel this good? I wonder.'

Without waiting for him to reply, she pushed the candle into the well of her vagina. It slid in smoothly and silently, eased in by the slickness of her secretions. Deeper and deeper . . . it didn't feel at all like a man's penis; more like a robot's sex-organ, cold and mechanical, excitingly different. 'Ah. Ah yes. That feels amazing. I wish you could feel it, Gabriel. I wish you could feel how wet I am.'

Gabriel did not speak. He was fascinated by this young Englishwoman, so well-bred and so wickedly sensual. It surprised him to realise that watching her masturbate excited him almost as much as having sex with her. If only his hands were free . . .

'Untie my wrists,' he begged her.

'Why? So that you can touch me?'

'So that I can touch myself. You're driving me crazy, can't you see?'

'Good. But you can get a little crazier before I untie you. Just lie still and watch.'

This unique sensation of power stimulated her like no other aphrodisiac. Suddenly she was all-powerful, all-knowing, the personification of sexual desire. The candle was her lover, her helpless male, filling her up at her whim, doing only what she commanded it to do. This was a fantasy made real . . .

As she masturbated slowly and luxuriously with the candle, her right index finger sought out the white-hot pleasure-centre of her sex. It felt hard, hyper-sensitive: so sensitive that she could hardly bear to touch it. Even the merest breath seemed to send knife-blades of pleasure through her whole body.

Scooping up a little of her own moisture, she used it to lubricate her clitoris and the delicate folds which half-concealed it. With a circular motion, she began to stroke and tease, coaxing the luxury of self-pleasure from her overheated body, easing herself towards a long, self-indulgent, perfect climax.

Her eyes drank in Gabriel's discomfiture: the painful hardness of his cock, its tip dripping glittering juice onto his belly; the tautness of every muscle; the hoarse, staccato rhythm of his breathing. He couldn't take his eyes off her fingers, working like an artist's, creating a perfect sculpture in flesh. A sculpture of purest pleasure.

A familiar tension in her belly; a tingling sensation in her fingers and toes; a divine numbness which turned first to pins and needles, then to a great surging warmth beginning deep inside her . . . it was coming, coming, coming.

She threw back her head, completely uninhibited now, forgetting even that Gabriel existed. She was alone with her own need, her own quest for the summit of delight.

'Come, Venetia. Go on, do it, do it, do it.'

Gabriel's voice tore into her consciousness at the very moment when her fingers awoke the first thrill of orgasm. And seconds later she was tumbling, falling, spinning down through the sparkling, scented air; carried away on a wild spring tide.

Sweet honeydew dripped down the inside of her thigh, sparkling against her golden skin. Still dizzy with excitement, she withdrew the candle. It glistened in the rose-pink lamplight.

'Taste me,' she breathed. And she knelt over Gabriel, sliding the candle-shaft over his parted lips.

He put out his tongue and tasted. The wax had melted a little, and its redness mingled with the powerful, sweet elixir of Venetia's womanhood. He had never tasted anything more delicious in his whole life.

Venetia bent over him and kissed him, her lips now imprinted with the scent of her sex and the dripping redness of the candle. Without saying a word, she sat up, then slid herself forwards until she was kneeling directly over Gabriel's face.

She heard his indrawn breath; a desperate, blissful shudder. Then she felt his face pressing into the hot, moist space between her thighs. His tongue darted into her like a serpent's, instinctively seeking out the well-spring of her desire. Her orgasm had not sated her; it had made her still more hungry, and she moaned with delicious pleasure as Gabriel's tongue and teeth re-awakened the throb of unsatisfied desire.

'You . . . surprised me last night,' commented Gabriel. He and Venetia were sitting, side by side, in the back seat of Gabriel's chauffeur-driven Mercedes, heading into the souk quarter and the medina.

'Really? You didn't enjoy it then?'

Venetia turned away and looked out of the window at the teeming streets of the city. It was difficult to look Gabriel in the face, after what had gone on the night before. Her head ached slightly, the legacy of too many bottles of champagne; but her body was still warm with the afterglow of a long night's lovemaking.

'I didn't say that.'

Gabriel laid his hand gently on Venetia's thigh and stroked it through the thin, floaty cotton of her summer dress. She did not push him away, yet neither did she respond. She was confused about her feelings for Gabriel Engelhart. How was it possible to be sexually attracted to a man she didn't like? How could she feel so little and so much, all for the same person?

'What then?'

She forced herself to turn and look at him. He looked very Aryan and just a little frightening, with his glittering blue eyes and wavy, naturally blond hair.

'You realise I shall make you pay the price?'

He spoke the words casually, as if they were a joke, but Venetia thought she felt something else there, something dark and distant. Something she'd rather not know about.

'Do you have to talk in riddles?' she asked, with apparent playfulness.

'It is quite simple. You made a slave of me for one night,' he replied with complete frankness. 'That was our bargain, wasn't it? Well, now it's my turn. How are you going to repay me?'

Suddenly Gabriel's hand felt heavy, sticky and unpleasantly hot on her thigh. Venetia wriggled free of it, and slid a few inches away from him on the polished leather seat. She felt hot and uncomfortable in her modest, long-sleeved, long-skirted summer dress.

'Don't play games with me, Gabriel.'

'I never play games. I'm deadly serious.'

'I don't owe you anything.'

'True.' Gabriel smoothed back his blond mane, and the diamond cufflinks glittered with an unforgiving brilliance. 'But you have agreed to work for me. And Dr Hale is counting on you to save the project. You wouldn't want to let him down now, would you?'

This time she met Gabriel's gaze.

'Don't try to blackmail me, *Mister* Engelhart. I'm nobody's plaything. Just because I find a man attractive and spend a few nights with him, that doesn't mean I belong to him.'

Gabriel held his hand up, conciliatory again.

'Of course not.' His eyes were dark shadows in his pale face. 'I would never try to make you do anything you didn't want.' He smiled. 'But you do want me, don't you Venetia?'

Venetia chose to ignore Gabriel's question. She looked out of the window, at the teeming horde of colours, the meeting of East and West. They could only drive very slowly through the crowded street, and occasionally, a child's face pressed up against the car window, the mouth opening and closing on the other side of the glass, offering some gewgaw or trinket for sale.

'Where are we going?'

'Through the medina and into the *souk des libraires*. Yusuf has a shop there.' Gabriel tapped his chauffeur on the shoulder. 'Pull in over there. We will walk the rest of the way.'

Venetia stepped out of the car and into a noisy, jostling mass of men, women, children and dogs. There were even a few chickens scuttling around the market stalls.

At the very first glance it was clear that the medieval medina was very different from the

58

modern face of Tunis. Instead of concrete tower blocks there were white domes and minarets, and tunnel-like bazaars. In between stood magnificent doorways: the doors painted blue and beige with black studs and 'Hand of Fatima' knockers, and the whole surrounded by intricately carved stone frames.

'Quaint, isn't it?' commented Gabriel.

'It's full of character.'

'Oh, it's that all right. But come here alone, after dark, and you could find a knife between your shoulderblades. That's the beauty of the place: there's always an exhilarating undercurrent of danger.' He took hold of Venetia's elbow. 'This way.'

Venetia followed, glancing to left and right. She had been in North Africa before, and expected to feel hands roaming over her body, pulling away her light scarf to touch and stroke her hair. Eyes followed her, but from a respectful distance; and it wasn't difficult to see why.

When Gabriel spoke, people got out of his way. If they were too slow, a single look had them cowering: 'Yes, master, so sorry master.' There was something at once disturbing and admirable about Gabriel Engelhart.

'You're well-known in Tunis?'

'I have had a house here for five or six years. I do quite a lot of business in North Africa. Arabs are resourceful people. They can find anything, anywhere – for the right price.'

'Which is how you found out about Yusuf?'

Gabriel shook his head.

'I heard about Yusuf when I was travelling in Tehran – a distant cousin of his was useful to me.

Apparently Yusuf has an Arab's eye for aesthetic beauty, and a Persian mystic's taste for the erotic arts.' Pushing a group of street urchins out of the way, he led Venetia into a narrow alleyway between a textile shop and a bread-seller's stall. 'Here we are. The *souk des libraires*.'

A plaque on the wall proclaimed in Arabic and English: 'Yusuf Akhbar, Treasures and Secrets.'

Gabriel rang the bell, and a small boy came to let them in. The shop itself was rather dark, and extremely small, lit only by a single window which looked out onto a back courtyard.

Yusuf emerged from behind a pile of antique rugs, books and furniture. About fifty years old, with a silky greying beard and embroidered cap, he came forward with a smile of welcome.

'Greetings sir, madam. You have come to buy a fine carpet, perhaps a beautiful book – or a trinket for the lady?' He cast an appreciative eye at Venetia. 'Come into the inner room and my boy will serve us coffee while we talk . . .'

Gabriel shook his head. 'There is no time for coffee. There is something we must discuss with you. Something very important.' Taking his wallet from his back pocket, Gabriel laid several high-denomination bills on the table. 'Your cousin Mukhtar sent us to you. He tells me you have information.'

'Information, sir? What manner of information? I am but a humble merchant.'

Venetia stepped forward.

'My name is Venetia Fellowes, Mr Akhbar. I am an archaeologist, an expert in ancient languages and manuscripts. My . . . colleague Mr Engelhart believes that you may know of the whereabouts of the *Lore of Madali*.'

Yusuf paled visibly, even in the twilight. Placing his finger to his lips, he shook his head.

'Please, madam. Do not speak its name here. There may be others watching, listening.' Crossing to the window, he closed the shutters then clicked on a dingy yellow electric light.

'But surely – this book – it doesn't even exist,' protested Venetia. 'I have never seen any evidence to suggest that it is more than a romantic legend.'

Yusuf and Gabriel exchanged glances. It was Gabriel who spoke first.

'In your heart, you know the book exists, Venetia. You are as driven as I am by this quest.'

Venetia cleared a spot on Yusuf's desk and perched on the edge.

'You have information, Mr Akhbar?'

Yusuf's eyes met Gabriel's for confirmation. Gabriel nodded.

'You have my word that I will make this worth your while, Mr Akhbar.' He laid more banknotes on the table. 'More than worth your while.'

Yusuf seemed uncertain for a moment, then took a key from under a heap of dusty books and disappeared into a back room. Moments later, he returned carrying a leather portfolio tied with green string. He unfastened it with extreme care, the old leather creaking in protest as he laid it flat on the table. He looked up.

'You must know, such things as these are forbidden in this country. If anyone knew that I possessed this . . .'

Gabriel offered no assurances, his blue eyes holding Yusuf prisoner. 'Show us what you have.'

Hesitantly, Yusuf opened up the portfolio.

Inside lay a single black and white photograph, yellowed with age and curled at the edges. But the image itself was crystal clear: the image of a book, laid open at a double page to display words and pictures, riotous images of beautiful men and women, mythical beasts, coupling together in a garden of breathtaking beauty within a strange and wonderful city. It was obscene and exquisite, imaginative and explicit.

Venetia was struck dumb by the beauty even of this single photograph. It was Gabriel who cried out in triumph, seizing it and examining it minutely.

'This is it,' he muttered under his breath. 'It must be, it must . . . everything is as I had imagined it would be.'

Venetia looked over his shoulder, tracing the words and pictures with her fingertip; translating slowly, painstakingly.

'This page is written in medieval Latin,' she said. 'It's very corrupt, but I can just make it out. It says, "Oh my love, my flower of the citrus tree, your lips upon my penis are as the softness of the butterfly's wings . . ." There are other things too, things I don't understand in a language I don't recognise. And funny symbols I've never seen before.' She traced them with her fingertip, her heart thumping with the excitement of discovery. Could this really be a page from the *Lore of Madali*?

Gabriel let the photograph fall and turned to Yusuf, seizing a fistful of his long, white jellabah. 'Where is it? Tell me, Yusuf, I will pay you anything. Anything, do you understand?'

Very afraid now, Yusuf pulled away, shaking out the creases in his robes. He took a step back. 'I have told you all I know. I have told you more than it was right or wise to tell.'

'You must know more. You *must*.'

'The picture is all I have, I swear it. Only this, and things I have heard, nothing more than rumours . . .'

'Tell me.' Gabriel's voice offered no chance of refusal.

'They say . . . it is said that the different paintings and inscriptions were found and bound together by the magician Paulus Madalinus, around the year 1590 – legend has it that the leather binding bears his sign: a star within a circle, stamped on the upper outer corner of the book.'

'But where, Yusuf? Tell me where the book is.'

Yusuf shrugged. He looked uneasy and fearful. Venetia felt uncomfortable too, torn between the desire to know more and a fear that Gabriel's obsession would drive him beyond reason.

'That is all I know.'

Venetia touched Yusuf's forearm. He jumped, as though stung.

'Please, Mr Akhbar. Tell us all you know. It is important.' Important to me, pleaded her eyes. He looked away. 'There have been rumours that the book is in Eastern Syria. Is that true?'

Yusuf turned back towards her and shook his head. 'No. Perhaps once, but not now. Not for a long time.'

'Then where?'

Yusuf hesitated, then gave a sign of resignation. 'Cairo,' he replied. 'I heard that it was seen there, not six months ago.'

When Venetia emerged from Yusuf's shop and into the *souk des libraires*, darkness had fallen. The streets, which before had been crammed full of people and noise, were now almost deserted. Only a few nameless shadows walked away into the distance, ignoring the two figures in European dress, and the shop door grating shut behind them.

'Come on. The driver will be waiting to take us back to the house. It isn't safe here after dark.'

Venetia did not move. It felt as though a cold, ethereal hand had stroked its transparent fingers down the back of her neck. She shivered.

'What is the matter with you, Venetia? Come on.'

She turned back to Gabriel, and they walked on together. But as she left the souk, she turned and looked over her shoulder, certain that she must see someone, or something, half-hidden by the darkness. A shape. A shadow . . .

And yet there was nothing there.

So why did she feel so convinced that someone was watching her, someone who had waited for her for a very long time. . .?

Chapter Four

IN THE VELVETY darkness of a North African night, Venetia was dreaming.

At first, she did not realise that she was dreaming at all. It seemed so real.

Venetia was naked; lying on soft, damp grass in the cool of a summer's evening. She was in a forest; a great, piney glade with whispering branches which arched overhead, criss-crossing to form a high canopy. Somewhere nearby, she could hear cicadas singing in the trees. The air was still, scented, clear as springwater.

It was many, many years ago, of that she was certain. How long? Her fuzzy, dreamy brain would not quite click into focus. Why was she here? And where was 'here'? And who was this lover whose kisses carpeted her body, his skin cool as sculpted stone?

She moaned as his lips traced a slow path down her belly to the soft mound of her pubic hair. He took her outer labia into his mouth, kissing and sucking them, so that the hood of her clitoris slid back and forth, provoking irresistible sensations that made her forget all the questions tumbling round and round in her head.

He did not speak, yet it was as if she could hear his every thought inside her head.

'*Toi seule, petite anglaise*. You alone . . .'

Fleetingly, she felt afraid, wanted to push him away, but he held her tightly, pressing his face into the fragrant glade of her sex, sucking and licking at her womanhood. She climaxed again and again, the pleasure seeming to go on and on, never ebbing away, only growing and swelling like her need for this man.

'Do not fear me, Venetia. Why do you fear me?'

His body slid over hers and she raked her nails down his back. She heard him growl his pleasure, then he kissed her full on the mouth, with a savage, tender passion which took her breath away. She wanted to scream, to cry, to hold him for ever and never let him go.

His lips tasted of her own sweetness, and of some far-distant, half-remembered ecstasy. At last, as he drew away and began to kiss and lick her throat, she understood.

'Esteban . . .!'

The breath escaped from her in a low, moaning cry. He hushed her again with his kisses, not speaking but holding her very tightly as his penis slid inside her. She felt the smooth stone ring which pierced his glans as it stretched the delicate, sensitive walls of her womanhood; tasted his sweat, breathed in the essence of him as their hunger joined and grew to fill the whole world.

From the velvet-dark sky above them, soft, warm rain began to fall on their joined bodies,

66

trickling over their skin, bathing them like the world's tears.

Pleasure and pain ... there was nothing between the two, not so much as a hairsbreadth. Venetia could no longer judge between the two, no longer understood which was good, which bad. She felt Esteban climax inside her, thrilled to the twist and jerk of his penis, heard the long, low gasp as his strength became utter vulnerability; surrendering for a few, brief moments to the dominion of ecstasy.

Her own orgasm swelled within her suddenly, a chorus of pleasure rising to a scream of remorse as the last, warm ache died away and she felt Esteban pull away from her.

'No, Esteban. No, don't leave me. Come back.'

He got to his feet. She saw him in the half-darkness, his face exactly as she remembered it, only more beautiful and more sardonic. The aristocratic, aquiline profile, the mane of collar-length dark hair, the diamond-black eyes that saw into her very soul. His lips were moist with her elixir, and as he wiped them on the back of his hand Venetia remembered that this should not have happened. This was impossible, dangerous, insane. Impossible because Esteban was not like other men. Esteban was neither living nor dead.

Esteban was a vampire.

She watched him put on his armour: the chainmail tunic, the crusader's tabard that hung loosely on his tall, slim-hipped frame from broad shoulders, the sword thrust through the leather belt. And for the first time, he spoke.

'It is time. I must leave you now.'

'No, Esteban. Don't go. I need to understand . . .'

'I have no choice. You know this cannot be.'

He mounted the great, grey stallion lightly. Venetia got slowly to her feet. The first glimmerings of dawn were visible as a dark-blue haze on the horizon. An ache of longing filled her, and she heard herself cry out: 'Let me come with you.'

'Where I dwell, no mortal may follow.'

She met his eyes; such beautiful, compelling, coal-dark eyes; so often burning with anger or arrogance or contempt, now empty save for a kind of sadness.

'Stay. I don't understand. Stay . . .'

But Esteban shook his head slowly and, spurring on his horse, disappeared through the forest, into the night.

Venetia awoke confused, not certain if she was awake or still dreaming. Then she remembered. She was alone in the big carved bed in Gabriel Engelhart's guest room, a scented wind wafting in through the open window.

Opening her eyes, she blinked in astonishment, fear, perhaps just a glimmer of hope. For Esteban was standing at the foot of her bed, dressed as she had known him in Valazur: tall and rangy in his long black jacket and trousers, and embroidered silk waistcoat. Every inch the professional gambler, the mysterious figure in black.

She sat up, breathless with hope. 'Esteban. Esteban, I . . .'

'Beware, Venetia. Beware Engelhart. Trust no one . . .'

Scrabbling for the switch, she turned on the bedside lamp. Orange-yellow light filled the room; and Venetia saw how she had deceived herself. Esteban was not there. He had vanished. He had never been there at all.

A tear of disappointment escaped from the corner of her eye, and she rolled sideways, clutching at the pillow for comfort. As she did so, her fingers made contact with something soft and fragile. Propping herself up on her elbow, she picked it up and stared at it, shaking, disbelieving.

Beside her, on the pillow, lay a single thornless rose – the colour of freshly-shed blood.

Showering and dressing in a satin robe, Venetia went downstairs in search of Gabriel.

Outside, the heat would already be mounting, the North African sun sizzling the dusty mud-bricks and concrete of the city. But inside Gabriel's townhouse it was perpetual spring. The high-ceilinged, marble-lined rooms lent the house an airy, spacious feel; and the discreet air-conditioning kept the temperature cool enough for comfort, warm enough for the barest minimum of clothing.

There were flowers everywhere. Great drifts of jasmine and tropical creepers tumbled from hanging baskets and terracotta pots, forming bright-green curtains of foliage, spangled with scented flowers. Their perfume was at once fresh and heady, filling Venetia's head with dreamy thoughts of a faraway summer land, gentler by far than this harsh climate.

She walked down the broad, curving central staircase and into the entrance hall. The sunken fishpond glittered with the gold and silver shadows of fish, the water constantly rippled and renewed by a hidden underground spring which bubbled up through the polished floor.

Ismail bowed to her as she passed. Everything he did was executed with the utmost respect, and yet she could not bear to be near him. She found him creepy, too obsequious to be sincere.

'Good morning, Ismail.'

'Good morning, madam.' Ismail's head was bowed, but he was looking up, his dark eyes fixed covetously on her. Suddenly selfconscious, Venetia looked down. Her robe had fallen slightly open at the front, baring the tops of her breasts and one long, golden thigh. Small wonder Ismail looked distracted. Colouring up with embarrassment and annoyance, she adjusted her robe.

'Where is Mr Engelhart?'

'The master is . . .' Ismail coughed, as though faintly embarrassed. 'He is in the . . . er . . . kitchen.'

Venetia looked at him in surprise. Ismail explained.

'It is a fancy of the master's, madam. He does not like to be disturbed in the mornings, and so he likes to prepare his own breakfast. It is not fitting,' he added under his breath.

'Had I better not disturb him, then?'

For the first time, she thought she caught the shadow of a smile on Ismail's thin lips. A rather bitter little smile, she thought to herself.

'Madam, he shuns me, but I am quite sure he will be delighted to see *you*.'

Ismail indicated the passageway which led to the kitchens, and Venetia set off along it, wondering how many more surprises Gabriel Engelhart had in store for her.

The corridor was lined with small alcoves, each one housing a statuette, painting or mosaic. Unlike the Moslems he lived among, Gabriel was not constrained by strict religious conventions which dictated that art must never depict the human face or form. On the contrary, it was clear that Gabriel was more than appreciative of physical beauty . . .

This place was a treasure trove of artefacts from every race and time, every corner of the globe. There were carved wooden fertility statuettes from West Africa, their phalluses and breasts hugely exaggerated; fragments of a Roman mosaic pavement, depicting an orgy in which naked dancers cavorted with satyrs in an orange grove; a priceless sixteenth-century erotic miniature, 'Love's Awakening'; even an unknown Egyptian bas-relief, representing the Pharaoh as both male and female, enjoying the delights of his concubines and his serving-boys.

Venetia was beginning to understand now that money could mean very little to a man like Gabriel Engelhart. He had all the money he could ever need, and then some. No, what mattered to him now was the challenge of finding something that nobody else had got.

That must be the reason why Gabriel Engelhart was so desperately keen to get his hands on the *Lore of Madali*. And if – or when – he did, he would move on to the next challenge, hungry for another quest to bring excitement into his predictably successful life. Venetia wondered for a moment if she had been a challenge too: an acquisition he had made up his mind to have. And now he had her, what next?

71

Reaching the end of the corridor, she hesitated, then pushed open the door. Gabriel was sitting in the middle of the kitchen, at an enormous circular wooden table set with a jumble of fruit, meat, jugs of fruit juice, a dish of fresh *ftairs* and an unopened bottle of white wine, the chilled glass frosted with condensation.

He turned to greet her.

'Ah, Venetia. I was wondering when you would come and join me.'

Venetia stepped inside and closed the door behind her. She was standing in a large, old-fashioned kitchen with whitewashed walls and lots of carved, dark wood. From the beams above her head hung sides of cured and spiced meat, game birds, long strings of garlic and bunches of herbs. Mellow morning sunshine flooded the room from windows set high in the walls, their ornamental metal grilles casting complex patterns wherever the light fell.

'When did you wake up?' asked Venetia, accepting a glass of orange juice and sliding onto a chair at the table.

'Oh, around four.' Gabriel shrugged. 'I don't need a lot of sleep. My mind's very active.'

'Not just your mind, as I recall.' Venetia failed to suppress a smile.

'No.' Gabriel stroked her throat and she leaned back, her hair falling behind her in a long, glossy curtain. He kissed a long line from chin to breastbone, making her shiver with appreciation. 'But I don't recall you complaining.'

He turned back to the pile of food on the table.

'What would you like? I am an excellent cook.'

'And modest with it?'

'Modesty is an affectation,' replied Gabriel. 'What is the point of pretending to be any less than you are?' He picked up a physalis dipped in white chocolate, peeled back the calyx and dangled the fruit so that it was just touching Venetia's lips. She put out her tongue and licked it, and he let it slide into her waiting mouth. It tasted good; a mixture of sweet and sour, smoothness and acid juice.

He licked the juice from her lips and they kissed, his tongue exploring the last traces of juice and melted sugar glaze.

'What shall I cook you?'

'Your choice.' Venetia leaned back. 'This is luxury, having a handsome man cook breakfast for me. What do you recommend?'

Gabriel wrinkled his nose. 'Not the local food, that's for sure. *Brik à l'oeuf* is impossibly vulgar, and *draw* is just plain tasteless. How about a soufflé omelette stuffed with fresh strawberries soaked in champagne?'

'Mmm. Sounds heavenly.' She pushed back her hair, breathing in the soft scents of fruit, herbs and spices. 'You know, this is dangerous. I could get used to being spoilt.'

She watched Gabriel cooking, genuinely impressed by his confident skill as he whisked egg-whites into a featherlight fluff, and folded them into the omelette mixture. The aroma of the lightly-frying omelette was sweet and sensual. On impulse, she got to her feet and walked over to where Gabriel was standing. Standing behind him, she slid her arms about his waist.

Breakfast she could live without, thought Venetia; but she *was* hungry. A wicked little stirring in her belly reminded her that it had been – oh, hours and hours . . .

She nuzzled into the back of his neck and bit him; just gently, hardly enough to feel it. But he responded instantly, turning round and taking her into his arms, pushing his belly up against hers; proving to her that his need was every bit as great as hers.

His strong hands smoothed down her back and found the rounded curves of her backside, cupping and squeezing the firm flesh. Venetia put her hands round Gabriel's neck and pulled his face down to hers, forcing a kiss on his lips, ignoring the bristliness of his unshaven chin.

Both were panting when the kiss ended. Gabriel looked at Venetia with a lopsided grin. He nodded towards the still-sizzling frying pan, and the fluffy golden omelette.

'We'd better eat before it gets cold.'

'I guess.' A note of regret entered Venetia's voice. Their eyes met, the shared thought passing between them. Then Gabriel arranged the omelette and the strawberries onto a plate and they sat down like two civilised dinner party guests.

'Only one plate?'

Gabriel's gaze met hers.

'You object to sharing?'

'Of course not.'

He speared a strawberry on his fork and held it out for Venetia to taste. She parted her lips and took a bite from it. It was very, very cold; the sharpness of chilled champagne mingling with the sweetness of strawberry juice and the faint bite of white pepper.

As she bit into the berry, the juice sprang from the flesh and trickled down over her lips and chin.

'How very messy,' murmured Gabriel, leaning forward and licking away the clear pink trickle of juice. He chuckled. 'It makes you look like a vampire.'

For a split second, a frisson of unwelcome memory ran over Venetia's skin. No, no; she would not think about Esteban. She must not. He had belonged to a faraway time, a time before she had known who and what he was. And besides, she had never really cared for him. She was just deluding herself if she believed it had ever been more than a casual dalliance.

She forced herself back to the present, and scooped up a spoonful of omelette. Gabriel took it into his mouth, then kissed her, forcing her to share the taste and the texture.

She pulled away, gasping with laughter, wiping her hand across her sticky mouth.

'Animal,' she teased.

'Come here and say that.' His eyes sparkled with merriment. A savage pleasure which half-excited, half-frightened her.

'Come here and make me.'

He caught her and, to her surprise and alarm, picked her up in his arms. It was only now that she realised just how strong Gabriel Engelhart really was.

'Put me down.'

'You told me to make you, and so I am.'

'Put me down. I'll scream!'

'Fine, scream. No one will disturb us, not even Ismail. I'm sure he told you how much I hate to be disturbed at breakfast.'

She looked into his piercing blue eyes. He was playing with her, as a cat plays with a baby bird; taunting her, knowing only too well how much his arrogance maddened and excited her.

He tossed her over his shoulder, as though she had no more dignity than a sack of potatoes, her backside in the air and her fists drumming on his broad back.

'I suppose you think I *like* being treated like this?'

'Of course you do,' replied Gabriel smoothly. 'You're a woman. A very sexy woman,' he added, giving her bottom a hefty thwack.

She wriggled in his grasp, but both of them knew he wasn't going to let go until he was good and ready. Venetia wasn't even sure she wanted him to, though she was mad as hell with him for this act of pure machismo.

With his free hand, Gabriel found the belt which held Venetia's robe closed at the waist, and untied it, letting the silky strip slither to the tiled floor. Her robe hung loosely now, just a thin veil of pale blue satin between her flesh and his desire.

'You're a haughty bitch, Venetia Fellowes,' breathed Gabriel. 'A bitch and a prick-tease, do you know that?'

Through the satin robe, his fingers traced the deep furrow between Venetia's buttocks. She made no lucid reply, only letting out a low moan, halfway between outrage and ecstasy.

'The way you behave, it's a wonder you don't drive men mad.' Gabriel's voice became husky with excitement. 'The other night, when we first arrived here, I let you play your little game. It excited you, and it excited me too, to play along for a while. But it's high time you knew your place, my high-bred English filly.'

This time he landed a hearty slap on her backside, making it jump and quiver. It smarted, *really* smarted; and Venetia let fly with a stream of curses.

'Tut, tut, Venetia. And I was so sure you were a lady,' said Gabriel reprovingly. 'It's obvious I shall need to teach you some manners.'

Pulling up the skirt of the satin robe, Gabriel bunched it up around Venetia's waist. She was bare now; the pale golden smoothness of hips, buttocks, thighs and legs completely at his will.

Venetia had never felt so exposed in her life before. She wasn't accustomed to being treated like an object, but no matter how she kicked and wriggled Gabriel held her fast. He had the upper hand and he was obviously enjoying being in control – just as she had enjoyed her illusory feeling of power the other night, when she had tied him up with silken ropes and imagined that she had some sort of magical hold over him.

She dangled over his shoulder like one of the Sabine women, her long mass of corn-blonde hair tumbling down his back and obscuring her vision. She tried scratching at his back but he just laughed and shook her off, carrying her across the kitchen as easily as if she had been a tiny child.

The next thing she knew, Gabriel was letting go of her, and she was sliding down onto the hard, scrubbed surface of the huge circular table-top, sending pots of jam and dishes of fruit skidding in all directions. There was a tinkling sound as a serving-dish shattered on the floor, and the soft thud of a fresh-baked *pain rustique* bouncing off the tiles.

'You're good enough to eat, Venetia, do you know that?'

Gabriel's voice was low, dark and husky. Venetia, lying on her belly amid the mess of jam and squashed fruit, slewed her head round to stare up at him. His eyes glinted.

'Good enough to eat. So that's what I'm going to do.'

Venetia rolled onto her back, intending to slide off the table and walk away; but Gabriel had other ideas. He held her there, on her back, and admired what he saw. The blue satin robe was hanging open on the right side, and was soaked through in patches, rendering it almost transparent as it clung to Venetia's skin. Pink strawberry juice had soaked into it where it passed across her left breast, and the large, pink, semi-erect nipple showed clearly through the wet fabric. Lower down, cream and fragments of crushed peach spattered the gown, making it hug the contours of lower belly and thigh; her golden pubic triangle shyly peeking from underneath.

Reaching out, Gabriel plunged his bare hand into a bowl full of whipped cream, scooping up a large handful. Bending over Venetia, he let great thick gobbets of the cream fall slowly and languidly onto her body, sometimes falling onto her gown, sometimes onto the bare flesh of belly and breast.

Venetia shuddered. The cream was straight out of the refrigerator, chilled so cold that it shocked her as it touched her skin with its icy kisses. Her left nipple contracted and hardened at the first touch, half in a reflex, half because, in spite of her anger, Venetia was finding this an exciting experience.

Getting up onto the table, Gabriel knelt over her. She found his expression a little frightening. He was looking at her with such intensity, as though he was thinking not so much of pleasure or of lovemaking, but of possession.

His hands ran over her body, smearing the whipped cream over her exposed breast and belly.

'This is all the clothing you need. This must go.'

He peeled the robe from her, the last shadow of modesty remaining to her, baring the moist, firm flesh beneath. And he bent down closer, taking yet more of the whipped cream and massaging it into her skin, leaving not a millimetre uncovered.

She stopped fighting him, and began writhing at his touch. It was too intense to be entirely pleasant, too relentless. There seemed to be no escape from the sheer force of his desire. And when he dropped a cold, cold mass of cream onto the hot triangle at the base of her belly, she let out a shrill wail of fearful pleasure.

'That's it, Venetia, admit it. Admit that it excites you.'

She wanted to deny it, to look coolly up at him and spit in his face, but it was all too cruelly true. She wanted nothing more than for this to go on, to become more and more outrageous and extreme.

'I knew it instantly, Venetia. For all your cleverness you're still a slut underneath.'

His hands took hold of her and flipped her back

onto her belly, face-down amid the breakfast debris. The opened bottle of champagne toppled sideways and a pool of cool, pale-yellow liquid spread out on the table-top. Gabriel picked up the bottle and upturned it, letting the champagne fall in a cool stream over Venetia's hair, shoulders, back and backside.

She shivered, not just with cold. There was something powerful and dark about Gabriel's desire for her; something she wasn't sure that she liked very much.

Cream, fruit, more wine. Gabriel poured and smeared her flesh with anything and everything that came to hand, insinuating the slimy mess into every secret crevice, watching with satisfaction as it oozed and trickled down over her bare buttocks and tight-clenched thighs.

'Now you're ready for me,' he whispered.

She turned her face sideways, looked up at him.

'You're an arrogant bastard, Gabriel Engelhart. What makes you think I want anything to do with you?'

He laughed, running the flat of his hand over her backside, then letting the very tips of his fingers slide into the deep crease between her buttocks.

'Because I can smell you, Venetia. You stink of sex.'

He stroked her back and flank almost lovingly, and she groaned with the irresistible sweetness of it. It was no use denying the need she felt, even if she was walking a narrow tightrope between being attracted to Gabriel Engelhart and despising him.

'You smell divine, you're my finest creation, do you realise that? And now I'm going to devour you . . .'

The first touch of his tongue was a long, sweeping stroke that ran from the base of her spine right up her back to the hollow between her shoulder-blades. Instinctively Venetia arched her back, rising and falling to the rhythm of each new stroke. He licked her as a cat laps at some delicious delicacy, his tongue hollowing to scoop up the mess of sweat and cream and crushed fruit, swallowing it down then returning to caress again and again.

'Don't . . . don't do that . . .' she murmured as he slid down her back and began licking and biting her buttocks.

A chuckle of mischievous delight rumbled through Gabriel's body. 'Why not?' he taunted her. 'Not afraid, are you?'

'I told you, I'm not afraid of you. I'm not afraid of anything.'

'Not even . . . *this*?'

A sudden intrusion between her buttocks made Venetia's whole body tremble, and she tried to wriggle sideways. But Gabriel was having none of it.

'Stay still. You might enjoy it. In fact, I guarantee you'll enjoy it. Or is that what you're afraid of, my beautiful English slut?'

Gabriel's fingers took hold of Venetia's buttocks and pulled them apart. This time, there was no false gentleness in his touch. He knew what he wanted, he knew what they both wanted. Why waste time on foolish preliminaries which would only bore them both?

She was beautiful. She was insatiable. He had known she would be. The tiny, tight rosebud of her anus was a delicious shade of amber beneath the fragrant slick of cream and fruit juice. Tenderly, he licked it away, revealing its unique and secret beauty.

'Bastard,' spat Venetia, her protest muffled as her face was pressed hard against the table-top. Her fingers scrabbled at the smooth surface, but to no avail.

'Hush. Just lie still.'

Gabriel knew many tricks to give a woman pleasure, to still her doubts and dislikes, and turn her to yielding devotion in his hands. He had had many women, every one of them a beautiful, sensual creature; but none had pleased him more than this fiery, sensual Englishwoman. He intended to enjoy taming her.

His fingernails grazed and scored the sensitive membrane of her anus, and he felt her shudder and squirm. Good. That was exactly as it should be. There could be no pleasure in the thing if the girl was entirely without inhibitions. And pleasure was always at its greatest when it contained some element of the forbidden.

Bending low over her, he pressed his face between Venetia's buttocks and breathed in the intoxicating scent of her: a carnal essence of sweat and sex, mingled with the freshness of cream and fruit.

Then he put out his tongue and, ignoring Venetia's muffled curses, thrust it deep, deep, deep into the adorable softness of her backside.

Venetia felt a single tear escape from the corner of her eye. How could she express the gnawing ache which always returned to torment her, at the very height of pleasure? How could she ever escape the knowledge that no lover, no matter how skilful, how attractive, how attentive, could ever be good enough?

Because none of them was Esteban.

It was two days later when Gabriel and Venetia boarded the plane that would take them to Cairo.

Travelling first-class and incognito, Gabriel was a very different proposition to the wild beast who had possessed her so roughly and made it clear that Venetia's path to pleasure was to do exactly as she was told.

Here, sitting next to her, feeding her with red caviare on tiny savoury biscuits, Gabriel was the image of the perfect gentleman: polite, romantic, even tender. Venetia wondered what demon was inside this man, to make him change like the wind from one second to the next. And she resolved that, as soon as her work for him was concluded, she would take the next flight back to Malta and get him right out of her life.

'You are looking very attractive today.' Gabriel took off his sunglasses and slipped them into the top pocket of his Armani jacket.

'Thank you.'

Venetia dabbed at the corners of her mouth with a napkin. She had decided to play it cool, not quite sure how to react to Gabriel's change of image.

'You enjoyed the caviare?'

'It was . . . fine. Very nice. Thank you.'

Venetia resisted the urge to tell Gabriel that showing off with expensive food and wine wasn't the way to win her over. He probably wouldn't understand what she was talking about anyway. Men like Gabriel Engelhart were always convinced that they could buy anything if they were prepared to pay a high enough price.

Gabriel took hold of her chin and looked at her with interest, head on one side.

'Not still angry with me, are you? I mean, that would be absurd.'

'You think so?'

'You *are* angry with me.' Gabriel let out a gust of laughter, as though he could hardly believe that anyone could be quite so immature. 'We *have* still got a long way to go, haven't we?'

Venetia's eyes glittered a warning.

'*You* can go where you like. I'm here to work, remember?'

Gabriel put the tips of his fingers together. She hated him when he did that. He looked so calm, like a psychiatrist about to tell her that all her problems would be cured if she just did everything he told her to do.

'Yes, of course you are. I like a woman with spirit,' he added, handing the food trays to the stewardess with a nod, and snapping the tables back into the seats in front. His hand slipped sideways until it was resting on Venetia's thigh. 'That's why I like you.'

Chapter Five

IT WAS ALL very well being told that the *Lore of Madali* might be in Cairo. The problem was, knowing where to look.

Venetia had spent a frustrating day trailing all over the city in pursuit of elusive 'sightings'. She'd been to the Museum of Egyptian Antiquities, the library at the American University, even the Cairo Synagogue, all to no avail. And the book dealers on 26th July Street had simply shrugged off her questions and tried to sell her cheap editions of the *Kama Sutra*.

And so she found herself walking down Talaat Harb on a suffocatingly hot evening, so footsore and weary that she felt like a sleepwalker in somebody else's dream.

Pushing her way through the crowd, she approached one of the many stand-up juice bars which were dotted at regular intervals along the busy street. The female assistant greeted her with an apathetic '*Masa' il-kheer*' and Venetia slid her money across the counter.

'*Nus w nus, min fadlik.*'

The girl filled a paper cup with a mixture of carrot and orange juice and plonked it down with a thud.

'*Afwan.*'

Venetia silently cursed Gabriel Engelhart as she sipped the cool liquid. Why should he sit on his backside in some nice air-conditioned hotel bar, while she did all the leg-work? And did she really care enough about the Maltese project to waste so much time in a fruitless search for something that didn't even exist?

She decided to give it one more go.

'Are there any secondhand book dealers around here?' she asked the assistant. The girl glanced up.

'What?'

'Book dealers. Or antique dealers.'

The girl answered with a look that said 'stupid English tourist'. She shrugged as she turned to serve another customer.

'There is the shop of Mohammed al-Manakh. On the corner of Hoda Shaarawi, near to Felfela's Restaurant.'

'Thank you. *Shokran.*'

Just this one shop, Venetia told herself as she walked along Talaat Harb and turned the corner into Hoda Shaarawi. At first she didn't even notice the antique shop. It consisted of little more than a door and a tiny window, crammed in between a café and an airline office. A small sign above the door read simply: 'Mohammed al-Manakh'.

Venetia walked towards the shop and pressed her face against the window. A jumble of objects lay right up against the glass. As she'd expected, most of it was rubbish, designed to lure in the tourist trade. Amulets, scarab rings, 'genuine' ushabti figurines and Canopic jars lay heaped up on top of multicoloured rugs and some very obviously fake manuscripts, cooked up last week in a basement sweatshop.

She was about to give up and walk back to the hotel when the shop door opened.

'*Assalaamu aleikum*.' A very ancient-looking, dried-up grasshopper of a man beckoned to her to enter. 'Greetings, madam. You will enter the house of Mohammed al-Manakh?'

'No . . . no, I don't think so.' Venetia had already given this one up as a bad job. And besides, Mr al-Manakh was positively creepy, with his crêpy tortoise neck emerging from the gaping collar of his white shirt. She smiled politely but turned to go. 'I'm sorry, no.'

'I have many beautiful things, many jewels.'

'I'm not interested in jewellery.'

The old man came a little closer. His eyes were small and dark and glitteringly bright, the only feature of his desiccated body which really looked alive.

'What is it you seek, madam? Mohammed will find it for you, Mohammed can find anything . . . for a price.'

I bet, thought Venetia. But what had she to lose by asking?

'I am looking for a book. A collection of very old manuscripts.'

Mohammed licked his lips with an unattractive, lizard-like motion. He smiled, sensing an imminent sale. Once he had her inside his shop he would be sure to sell her something.

'Mohammed al-Manakh has many ancient books, beautiful books. If you will please to come inside . . .'

Venetia hesitated on the threshold, then followed him into the shop. It smelt of coffee and mildew, and she started as a tiny green lizard scuttled away from under her foot.

'This book . . .' she began.

'Yes, yes, beautiful books. I will show you my beautiful books.'

Mohammed rummaged in drifts of paper, pulling out book after book, tattered parchments, the odd thing of some small value, but nothing of any interest to Venetia. She cut in, interrupting his sales pitch.

'It is a collection of pictures. Very old pictures. Very . . . erotic.'

Mohammed's face cracked into a leer.

'You like dirty pictures? Mohammed have many beautiful pictures to show you, pretty lady.'

Venetia dodged Mohammed's questing hand and thrust the photograph into his face. 'Pictures like these? Pictures from the *Lore of Madali*?'

Mohammed could not have looked more shocked if he had been struck by lightning. In a split second his expression changed from lascivious interest to fear, then anger; the blood draining from his face so that its deep walnut brown faded to a jaundiced yellow.

'Leave my shop! Begone!' To Venetia's astonishment, he began pushing her away.

'The *Lore of Madali*,' she insisted. 'You know where it is, don't you?'

'There is no such book.'

'If you know something, tell me – you will be

paid well.'

'I will not speak of such things, *you* must not speak of such things.'

Opening the shop door, Mohammed thrust her outside. He stood inside the shop, half behind the glass door as though he feared what the Englishwoman might do to him.

'I don't understand . . .' began Venetia, but Mohammed shook his head, closing the door on her with such force that the glass almost shattered in its frame. His gnarled fingers turned the shop sign from 'open' to 'closed'.

'I know nothing. Now leave. Leave and never return. And forget that you ever spoke of the *Lore of Madali*.'

Gabriel clenched his hand into a fist and thumped it on the rail of the balcony.

'I must have it!'

Venetia poured two glasses of *asiir limoon* and carried them out onto the balcony, handing one to Gabriel.

'Here, drink this. You look like you need to cool down.'

Gabriel drank the chilled lemonade in a single draught, wiping his hand across his mouth. 'Thanks.' He paused, then, 'I guess I shouldn't be taking it out on you.'

Venetia shrugged. 'You're paying me to do a job. If I don't do it to your satisfaction, I suppose you have a right to complain.'

Gabriel searched her face, puzzled by her coolness, irritated by her lack of response. He took the glass from her hand and set it down, seizing her by the shoulders so that she was forced to look him in the face.

'You are more to me than a paycheck, Venetia, you know that.'

'Oh yes, I was forgetting.' She returned his gaze with an ironically raised eyebrow. 'I'm also your little English plaything, aren't I? That was what you said, wasn't it? *Very* romantic.'

Gabriel let out his breath in a grunt of exasperation. 'That was a game, Venetia . . .'

'If you say so.'

'Don't tell me you didn't enjoy it.' He stroked the side of her breast, very lightly, and she knew that if he chose he could have her at his mercy once again. 'I *know* you did.'

Gently but firmly, she pushed him away. It took a good deal more effort of will than she cared to admit, even to herself. 'I think we should maybe forget the sex and keep this professional, don't you?'

Gabriel followed her back into the room and took her by the arm, turning her round. 'No, since you mention it, I don't.'

Venetia saw a kind of mad hunger in his eyes. In an instant she saw what was happening. Her very rejection of him was making her ten times more exciting in his eyes. There was nothing more erotic than something you couldn't have. She prised his fingers from her arm.

'Look Gabriel, I'm not your possession, not your plaything, not *your* anything. Do you understand?'

Gabriel's eyes narrowed slightly. 'Oh, but you want to be, don't you? You want to so very much.'

She had a crazy urge to grab him and shake

some sense into him. How could he simply close his mind to anything he didn't want to hear?

'What is it with you? Is this some kind of massive power trip? Do you have to own everything you touch?'

'Not everything. Just the things which I consider to be truly exceptional.'

'It's a nice chat-up line, Gabriel, but forget it. It won't wash with me, not any more. In case you've forgotten, I've seen what you're really like.'

Her words seemed to evaporate into the still, burning-hot air, incapable of leaving any mark on Gabriel Engelhart.

'Your breasts, for example, are certainly exceptional,' he whispered huskily, stroking his finger down Venetia's bare forearm.

'D-don't,' she spluttered, suddenly confused. She didn't want to feel like this, like some mindless rutting beast. She wanted to tell Engelhart where he got off, wanted to push this unclean desire out of her life.

'But you want me to.' Gabriel slid his arm round her waist and drew her close, his hand roaming downwards to smooth over the swell of her buttocks.

'No.'

She pushed him away, half-heartedly. He responded by kissing her.

'Don't you?' he repeated.

And this time he held her more tightly, so that the hard swelling of his manhood pressed against the base of her belly, reinforcing his message: I want you, I want you, I want you. And like it or not, you want me too.

'Bastard.' The word escaped from her as a juddering sigh, shaking her whole body. The word that signalled her submission.

Gabriel held her close, just stroking her again and again as if she were a pet animal, soothing her with kisses on her upturned face and bare shoulders.

'Hush, hush, everything's OK. I have you now. Everything's going to be just fine,' he repeated over and over again, weaving his mesmeric web of desire about Venetia.

Eyes half-open, she returned his kiss. Pleasure surged through her body at the heat of his touch, sweat trickling between her shoulder-blades and down into the small of her back.

'How is it that you make me want you?' she murmured. 'When you know I've made up my mind to be strong?'

'Some things are meant to be,' Gabriel replied. And he gathered her up in his arms, carrying her across to his downy-soft, king-size bed.

On their arrival at the hotel, Venetia had insisted on separate rooms. She'd been determined to resist Gabriel's advances and try to get their relationship back onto a professional footing. Gabriel, of course, had easily found a way round her insistence by booking a suite of rooms with interconnecting doors and balconies, making sure that temptation was never more than a footstep away.

Up till now, Venetia had been strong. She had kept her distance, done what she had to and no more. But now she could feel every last ounce of willpower ebbing away. Lazy, luxurious, erotic thoughts took over, echoing Gabriel's persuasive words: why not? Why deny yourself pleasure? Sex is a fundamental human need: why starve yourself of it? And the need flooded her whole being, taking over, turning her half-crazy.

They fell onto the bed together, hands roaming over each other's bodies, clutching and tearing at each other's clothes. Venetia clawed at the buttons on Gabriel's Dolce & Gabbana shirt. He scarcely seemed to notice or to care as the handsewn silk tore and the shirt fell open, baring his chest. He fumbled with his trouser belt, helping her unbuckle it, not wanting anything to get in the way of instant gratification.

Venetia pulled her halter-top off over her head, letting the hot, dry air caress her bare breasts. She reached down to unbutton her shorts but Gabriel was already tearing them open, tugging them down impatiently over her hips. She responded by unzipping Gabriel's flies and slipping her hand inside; thrilling with delicious wickedness as she discovered that he was naked underneath.

His bare flesh slid so easily between her fingers, as if it was the most natural thing in the world to want to masturbate him, caressing his stone-hard shaft with short, light strokes.

Breathing heavily now, Gabriel rolled onto his side so that they were facing each other, their naked bodies lightly glistening with a sheen of sweat. Gabriel tilted his pelvis back and forth, maddened by the butterfly softness of Venetia's caresses on his dick.

'Harder,' he panted.

'Patience is a virtue,' she teased him, her eyes flashing defiance. 'Don't you know that?' And she uncurled her fingers, releasing his shaft. A brutal ache of loss tore through him. He seized hold of her hand and carried it to his lips, opening his mouth and taking her index finger inside.

She squirmed and convulsed, taken aback by the powerful sensations Gabriel provoked as he sucked, licked and nibbled at her finger. As her mind drifted and hallucinated, she imagined that she had a penis, and Gabriel was sucking it, making it swell and harden, awakening it to whole new levels of sensitivity.

'Let go, Gabriel, let go.' She giggled crazily. 'Don't! It tickles too much.'

She tried pulling her finger from between his lips, but he wasn't giving up so easily. His eyes never left hers as he let her index finger escape, slick with wetness, only to capture her middle finger, swallowing it up to the hilt.

Her pulse raced, a cold shiver of excitement running from the nerve-centre of her hostage fingertip down along her wrist and arm until it joined the burning hunger in her belly. She writhed like a snake, but it was not until she lay very still, mesmerised by pleasure, that Gabriel let her escape from his tyrannical kiss.

He ran his tongue down from the tip of her index finger to the hollow of her palm, working the tip round and round as though he were massaging her with the slick wet head of his penis.

'You see, Venetia? I told you I know what you like. All you have to do is believe me. It's so easy.'

Easy. Yes, the easiest thing in the world, thought Venetia lazily, as Gabriel covered her breasts with tiny bites and kisses. Nothing could be easier than to give in to desire and do exactly what I feel. But at the last moment, Venetia's rebellious will kicked against her submission, and she pushed her lover away.

'I'm sorry, Gabriel, but no. I told you we should keep sex out of this. This is all wrong . . .'

Gabriel's expression changed. For a moment he looked almost concerned. 'Poor Venetia, you really don't understand yourself very well, do you?'

'Don't give me that! I understand myself well enough to know . . .'

'Shh.' His mouth covered hers, precluding all possibility of protest. Her body tensed, pushed against his, then fell back. It was useless. How could she tell him she didn't want him when it wasn't remotely true? Mentally, spiritually, emotionally, she loathed him. But physically . . . her poor body needed lust, desire, pleasure. It needed Gabriel Engelhart.

He slipped his thigh between hers and rubbed it against her pubic bone – gently, but just firmly enough to excite the half-swollen rosebud of her clitoris, making her own sweet juice well up from its ever-renewing spring.

Venetia responded by grinding her belly against the muscle-hardness of Gabriel's thigh, working herself up to a peak of burning, surging heat; bringing herself ever-closer to the crisis which had simmered inside her for too, too long. It felt good to know that if nothing else, she was in control of her own pleasure. And then, very close to the point of no return, Gabriel pulled away from her.

'You've had enough, I think.'

Venetia returned his gaze with a look of pure

95

loathing. 'What makes you so bloody sure that you know what I want?'

Gabriel ran his tongue up the side of her neck. 'I'm *sure* that you wanted to bring yourself off.'

There was something so dark, so very serious about Gabriel's words. Her eyes followed his hand as it reached out to the bedside cabinet and slid open the drawer. There was a jumble of colourful odds and ends inside – things she hadn't even realised were there.

'What . . .?'

Gabriel reached into the drawer and lifted out something very strange – something black and heavy, that jingled curiously as his hand closed about it.

'They're so perfect for you, Venetia. I had them made with you in mind. Aren't you flattered?'

Venetia gaped at Gabriel and edged slightly away. Something told her she had jumped feet-first into trouble. 'Look, I . . .'

Gabriel smiled as he kissed her and drew her back to him. 'Don't look so afraid. What's there to be afraid of?'

'Nothing – so let me go and get dressed.'

'No, no, no. You must learn to relax, Venetia. Look at them, aren't they the most beautiful things you've ever seen?'

He placed the things in her hand. She looked down at them, an icy shiver running like a cold finger down her spine. She was looking at a pair of medieval-style manacles, made from iron painted matt black and joined by a thick black chain.

'Put them on, Venetia.'

'You're joking!' She tried to thrust them back

into Gabriel's hands, but he closed her fingers over them.

'Try them. For me. How will you ever know the pleasure if you don't even try it?'

Venetia hardly knew how it happened. One moment she was shaking her head and telling Gabriel Engelhart that he could go take a hike; the next, he was fucking her so beautifully that all she could think of was the compelling need to thrust her backside against his belly and never stop . . .

'Oh. Oh, yes, yes,' she moaned as he drove into her, grinding her belly and nipples against the rough, embroidered linen bedspread as he took her from behind. His weight made the sensations brutal and sudden, squeezing and abrading them from her, making her cry out and scrabble with her fingernails on the wooden bedhead, helpless to escape the tyranny of her own pleasure.

When at last Gabriel allowed her to climax, she arched her back and roared with ecstasy, the wetness flooding out of her to form a dark, damp stain on the coverlet. In the dizzy afterglow she felt a light caress and then heard a metallic click.

'What . . . ?'

'It's what you want. I *know* it's what you want.'

Too late, she realised that Gabriel had taken advantage of her distraction to slip the manacles about her wrists. Her arms were gently imprisoned behind her back, rendering her almost helpless. Gabriel lifted her up and cradled her in his arms.

'You look breathtaking,' he whispered.

Venetia knew that she ought to feel fear – Gabriel was talking like a madman – but all she felt at this moment was excitement. Perhaps

Gabriel had been right after all. Perhaps all she really did crave, subconsciously, was to be his plaything, abdicating the responsibility for her own sexual satisfaction to his capricious will.

'Such a beautiful bondage,' Gabriel repeated, running his hands over Venetia's upturned breasts, their nipples erect and hard.

For all her unease, Venetia found her body responding to Gabriel's mad desire. The orgasm he had forced upon her had left her unsatisfied, craving more. Much more.

Gabriel stroked the back of her hair, kissing her forehead and her closed eyes. 'You make an exquisite slave.'

'I'm not your slave. I'm not anybody's slave.'

'Play the game with me, Venetia. Just this once. Let me show you what you're missing.'

Reaching into the drawer again, he took out a small glass jar. He unscrewed the top, and Venetia breathed in a curious, almost sickly scent, cloyingly sweet. It seemed to be a mixture of dozens of different perfumes – almond, chocolate, jasmine, orange blossom, patchouli, musk . . . As she watched, Gabriel used the creamy-white paste to anoint his penis.

'This is a gift for you, Venetia. A gift of perfect pleasure.'

Standing up before her, Gabriel took hold of Venetia's face, quite gently. She was not quite helpless. She could have struggled, but oddly, she didn't want to. The sweet aroma of the sticky white paste made her feel dizzy, light-headed, floaty . . .

As though by some secret reflex, her lips parted and she bent to take him into her mouth. He tasted good, obscenely good. His own scent mingled with the flower-sweet aromas of the unguent, melting on her tongue. Was the pleasure as strong for Gabriel as it was for her? She knew it must be, for she could hear him softly groaning, felt his shaft harden and twitch between her lips.

And that thought filled her with a lascivious joy. For even in bondage, there could be a secret power.

This little lust-fest really would have to stop, thought Venetia as she pushed and shoved her way through the Cairo streets. She didn't even like Gabriel Engelhart, let alone like him enough to want to play the obedient little sex-slave to his Caligula.

She was still at a loss to understand what it was that made her give in so easily to Gabriel's demands. And whatever else she felt for him, she knew she couldn't ever trust him. How many lies had he told her? How could she be sure that anything about him was what it seemed to be?

A deep feeling of unease ached in the hollow of Venetia's stomach. She sensed that there were hidden depths to Gabriel Engelhart; things she'd perhaps rather not know. He seemed to be able to exert an effortless power over people, things, money – and the longer she carried on working with him, the deeper she felt she was being pulled into the murky vortex of his life.

Yes, one thing was for certain; this would have to stop.

She walked on, past the big European stores and the pavement traders. It was good to be free of Gabriel for a few hours, but this afternoon she had drawn yet another blank. Despite the bizarre incident in the antique shop, she had unearthed precisely nothing of real value since they'd arrived in Cairo. Which was not improving Gabriel's temper, she reflected grimly as she spotted a pleasant-looking restaurant and headed towards it.

It was too hot to sit outside, and she stepped into the cool, twilit interior. It was crowded, a low hubbub of conversation subsiding suddenly at her arrival, then beginning again just as suddenly.

'Table for one, madam?'

'Yes, please.'

'You will dine in the ladies' section?'

Venetia met the waiter's gaze. She hated being banished to the back room with all the other women, convention or no convention.

'No, thank you.'

'But, madam . . .'

'No, thank you. I'll be fine in here.'

She was shown with some reluctance to a table by the wall. As her eyes grew accustomed to the twilight, she saw that the restaurant was stylishly decorated, and filled to the brim with curios of every kind – Arab embroideries, wall-hangings, shelves filled with ornamental brasses, horses' bridles, and pile after pile of old books, heaped up on shelves and tables around the diners.

As she ate grilled fish with okra, Venetia let herself relax a little. This wasn't a bad place at all: good food, decent air-conditioning, interesting decor – and no Gabriel Engelhart.

Venetia's gaze wandered to the pile of books on

a nearby shelf. She never could resist books, no matter how old, tatty or worthless. Scanning them, she identified that this batch were all three. Hardly surprising really. She looked away, then glanced back again, her gaze registering something, she wasn't quite sure what.

As she turned back to the books, she felt the hollow ache of excitement deep in her belly. No. Not here, in a downtown restaurant. It couldn't be. That would be just too silly for words.

But there was no denying the symbol tooled in gold leaf on the dark, age-worn leather: an ornate star within a circle, embossed on the upper outer corner of the binding.

She got to her feet and walked towards the shelves. Hands shaking, she reached up. But just as she was about to lift the book from the shelf, her hand met another. A man's hand. They touched, for an infinitesimal moment. Then drew away.

She swung round, and the blood drained from her face. She had not seen the man sitting there before, his table half-hidden by a carved wooden screen and potted ferns. As she watched, he took off his sunglasses and slipped them into the top pocket of his long, black jacket. Now that he stood beside her, his dark eyes challenging hers, his spare, athletic frame towering over her, she wondered how she could possibly have failed to notice him. His presence seemed to fill the whole restaurant.

'Esteban!' It could be no other.

The breath shuddered from her, the shock of seeing him again making her feel hot, cold, dizzy, afraid.

'I had not thought we would meet again.' Esteban's voice was quiet and calm, the hawkish features as cruelly beautiful as ever.

Venetia's fingers tightened about the book. She must remember why she had come here, chase these dark, seductive memories from her mind. But Esteban was quicker and stronger. He lifted the book down from the shelf. Venetia's mouth was dry with tension.

'Esteban, the book. Give it back to me.'

Esteban returned her gaze impassively. 'Why should I wish to give it to you, *petite anglaise*? It is what I have been searching for and at last I have found it.'

Venetia stared at him. 'The *Lore of Madali*? A medieval book of erotica? What would you want with a book of dirty pictures, Esteban? And just out of interest, what the hell do you think you're doing here?'

Esteban chuckled drily. 'I see that you are still the same Venetia.' There was a note of something soft, almost wistful, in his voice. 'Always so impulsive, so impetuous. Whatever makes you think I would be interested in a book of erotica? This is something very different.'

'I tell you, that is the *Lore of Madali*. It has Paulus Madalinus's sign on the cover, the star within a circle. Give it to me – I'll prove it to you.'

Seizing the book from Esteban, she laid it on the table and opened it. The scent of old parchment made her sneeze, and a single, dried flower fell onto the table top in a cloud of dust.

Venetia's face fell. There were no beautiful illuminated pages here. No erotic pictures. In fact, no pictures at all. Only page after page of tiny handwriting, spidery and brown with age.

'No . . .' She sighed and closed the book. 'I guess you were right. This isn't the *Lore of Madali*.'

She sat down heavily. Esteban remained standing, flicking idly through the pages. She looked up at his face. His expression had changed, his face drained of the confident anticipation which had seemed to fill him only seconds before.

'Is something wrong, Esteban?'

'This . . . is not what I was looking for.'

'And what is that?'

He shook his head.

'We agreed to part, Venetia. My existence need not concern you any further.'

His dark eyes met hers but she looked away. No, no, she pleaded in the silence of her thoughts. Don't let this happen to you again. Don't let him back inside your heart, your body, your life. He's not for you. Not for you, not ever.

She forced herself to look up at him, hating him with all the force of her being; hating him for being here, now, when she had fought so hard to forget him. 'Why are you here, Esteban? In Cairo?'

Esteban sat down opposite, pushing back the collar-length mane of his glossy, blue-black hair.

'Serendipity?' The ironic twist of his sensual mouth maddened Venetia.

'Don't bullshit me, Esteban. I want to know.'

'I have told you, I am looking for something. A book.' He ran his long, slender fingers over the dusty pages. 'But not, alas, this one.'

'You've been following me. Spying on me.'

This time, there was no irony in Esteban's

voice. 'Not spying on you, Venetia. Watching over you.'

'Oh yeah. Like you really expect me to believe that, do you?'

'It is for you to choose what you believe.' His fingers brushed hers, cool against her fevered skin. 'Be careful, Venetia. Be careful, he is dangerous. He is poison.'

'I don't need your advice, Esteban. I don't need anything from you. I thought I made that perfectly clear, back in Valazur.'

Suddenly afraid that she would not be as strong as she had to be, Venetia got to her feet. She shoved the old book across the table towards Esteban. 'Here, you take it. It's no bloody use to me.'

Turning away, she threw a handful of change onto the table and walked towards the door. Looking back over her shoulder, she called, 'And don't you dare follow me again. Don't even bloody well think about it.'

Yet, even as she walked out into the blazing sunshine, she could feel Esteban's cool, dark eyes on her; and the inexorable pull of need, whispering to her to fall back into his arms.

Chapter Six

VENETIA TURNED OFF the taps and swished the foaming waters with her hand, testing the temperature. Just right.

With a sigh of release she stepped into the bath and slipped into the water, luxuriating in the abundance of warm, fragrant bubbles swirling about her naked body.

Gabriel was nowhere to be seen, which was fine by Venetia. He was out somewhere making money, and at last she could relax. She reached out for her glass of chilled white wine and let a few drops linger on her tongue before savouring the frisson of delight as they slithered down her throat. Slowly the tensions began to ease out of her taut muscles, and she lay back, allowing herself to let go.

Her mind wandered. She was back in Valazur, on the pine-scented hillside above Esteban's villa. Somewhere below, she could hear the sound of surf crashing against rocks.

She lay with Esteban, her head cradled in the crook of his arm. He was whispering to her as he caressed her naked body.

'Stay, Venetia. Stay . . . it will be so easy . . .'

She let her hand skate over her own flesh, imagining it was Esteban's hand, daydreaming of the coolness of Esteban's lips as they closed over the aching, yearning crest of her nipple.

'One kiss, and life and death will have no more meaning. One kiss, and only our passion will exist. For ever . . .'

In her daydream it was dusk. In the dark-blue light she looked up and saw Esteban's eyes glow a lustrous, soft black. His hands smoothed over her body, awakening her body to a symphony of sensations. She sighed, and he bent to kiss her throat . . .

She moved in the warm bathwater, letting it explore her body, kissing the apex of her thighs, swirling about her back and legs. Rolling over onto her belly, she imagined that Esteban was stroking her back, darting cool, moist kisses from her neck to the base of her spine, floating with her in a deep-blue, tropical ocean.

Oh Esteban, she thought. Esteban, why did you follow me here? She remembered the night of their parting, when he had freed her from her obligation. She had sworn, if he helped her to rescue her twin sister, that she would repay him with the price of her soul, becoming a vampire like him, sharing his dark prison of eternity. But something in Esteban, some residue of nobility, had cared too much for her to force her to be his unwilling captive.

And so they had parted, Venetia walking away into the first pink shadows of the rising sun. Esteban had sworn that they would never meet again, yet here he was in Cairo; awakening so many memories and so many more fears and desires. Reminding her that he was the only man she had ever really cared about, enough to think of sharing eternity with him.

A sound made her open her eyes and look round. Her heart sank. Gabriel was coming into the bathroom – *her* bathroom – through the connecting door from his suite. She knew she should have locked the door.

He took off his cream linen jacket and slung it over the towel rail, then peeled off his shirt and kicked off his shoes.

'Mind if I join you?'

'Does it make any difference if I do?'

Gabriel frowned. 'Whatever's making you tense, there's no need to take it out on me.'

Unzipping his trousers and stepping out of them, he walked over to the bath and switched on the whirlpool. Bubbling, swirling eddies of warm, foamy water spurted hard against Venetia's body. It felt nice enough. But it would have felt nicer alone.

Gabriel got into the bath behind Venetia, and wound his legs around her hips. He began massaging her shoulders. She winced at the sudden raw ache.

'Mmm, you're tense, very tense. Bad day?'

'Oh, you know,' replied Venetia evasively. She had no desire to antagonise Gabriel again. 'How about you?'

'Nothing on the *Lore of Madali*. But I did a few deals, bought myself some *very* desirable Minoan curios, would you believe. They'll look fabulous in some rich idiot's penthouse. I'll charge him five times what they're worth and he'll think I'm doing him a favour.'

Venetia decided that she disliked him more than ever. 'You have no principles at all, have you?'

Gabriel grinned. 'Not so's you'd notice. Principles are for people who don't mind being poor.' He gave Venetia's backside an exploratory squeeze. 'You really must drop the holier-than-thou stuff, Venetia. You're missing out on all the best things in life.'

'I get by.'

'Ah, but I could make you . . . anything you want to be.'

'And all I have to do is exactly what you tell me, right?'

'Right.'

'Dream on, Gabriel. I'll screw you for the hell of it while we're out here, but become your slave for life? No way. I have more respect for myself.'

Gabriel changed tack. His hard cock-tip nudged suggestively between Venetia's buttocks. 'I want you,' he whispered.

'So?' Venetia tried to sound cool and in control, even though her heart was thumping.

'So I usually get what I want. Especially when it happens to be what the other person wants too.'

Looking away from him, Venetia could almost, but not quite, imagine that it was Esteban in the bath with her, Esteban's hands toying with her buttocks, Esteban's beautiful pierced dick pushing its way into the deep, wet furrow of her womanhood.

Venetia did not wait for Gabriel to make his next move. She offered up herself to the invader, taking it far, far inside her, engulfing it, imposing

108

the tyranny of her own pleasure upon it.

'Mmm, that feels good. You're a clever woman, Venetia.' Gabriel slid in and out of her with long, smooth strokes. 'Tell me about your fantasies.'

'My fantasies!'

'Your erotic daydreams, your castles in the air. What do you fantasise about when you want to make yourself come?'

The word 'Esteban' almost rose to her lips, but she swallowed it down. 'Making love on the beach. In the surf, right at the edge of the sea.'

'Tell me.' Gabriel pumped in and out of her with rhythmic precision, controlling everything, making her feel pleasure she didn't want to feel.

'You know, rolling over and over on the wet, pebbly sand, with the waves breaking right over me and drenching me as I fuck.'

'And what else?'

'Screwing in a mechanic's workshop.'

Gabriel chuckled. His fingers tightened on her buttocks. 'Go on.'

'The floor's all oily and muddy, and he's wearing these really old, tatty overalls. They're torn, and I can see his body through the holes. He's so strong . . . it's obvious he takes care of his body.'

'Really, Venetia? I can't say I'm surprised. Marcus Hale said you went for the brainless, musclebound type.'

His right hand slid round Venetia's belly and down into the thickly-forested glade of her sex. She knew he was playing her like some child's toy, and hated herself for going along with it. But it felt good and in any case, she was helpless to resist.

He slipped a finger between Venetia's thighs, sliding into her intimacy to toy mercilessly with her clitoris. She made no sound, but her body shook with need.

'Tell me more.'

'I . . . I've come to collect my car, but I can't afford to pay for all the work he's done. He . . .' She panted, finding it hard to control her breathing as lust took over her body as well as her thoughts. 'He tells me there's another way to pay . . .

'He touches me, and he leaves oily patches all over my best blouse. It's all dirty now, I'll have to take it off. And my skirt . . . I've torn it on a rusty nail, and there are ladders in my stockings.

'He helps me to undress. I can smell the oil and the sweat on him. His hair is full of grease, and there are black smears on his cheeks. When he kisses me I can taste engine oil and two-stroke. Somewhere in the background, I can hear motorbikes revving up, and I know there are other people watching us. Other mechanics, waiting for their turn . . .'

Gabriel growled with pleasure. He had known, instinctively, that Venetia Fellowes was the woman to satisfy his every desire – and Gabriel Engelhart didn't make mistakes. He made no apologies for being insensitive, even brutal at times; but he truly believed that he knew, better than any other man, how to give this sensual creature the pleasure she craved. And that knowledge gave him the right to exercise a unique power over her.

He had imagined her in a thousand different settings. Dancing naked for him at some desert oasis, bright jewels piercing her navel and nipples. Making mad love with him in some tropical lagoon, their bodies tumbling weightlessly in the water as their mouths met and drank in the elixir of their lust. Riding bareback on a half-broken stallion, her head thrown back and her mouth open in a silent scream of joy as the rough horsehair abraded her soft intimacy, torturing her flesh to the brink of orgasm. And now this new, seductive image, so fresh in his mind . . .

His penis tingled with the onrush of pleasure. With a massive effort of self-control, he managed to prevent himself climaxing. The mental picture of Venetia offering herself to this oil-smeared mechanic with his rough hands and tattered clothes was almost too much to bear. But he wanted to hear more.

'Tell me what you do next. *All* of it.'

Venetia felt light-headed, pleasantly wicked. She had never told anyone about her fantasies before. Somehow it didn't seem to matter if Gabriel knew.

'We're undressing each other. I'm so hungry for him, my fingers are all fumbling and useless. I can't get his buttons undone. His hands are stripping off my blouse, it's sticking to my skin with all the oil. And still I'm trying to undress him. I can't think of anything but the thought of what it will be like to see and feel him naked.

'He unfastens my skirt and I step out of it. It's a hot day and I'm not wearing any panties. So I'm standing in front of him wearing nothing but my bra, white stockings and suspenders, and high-heeled shoes. He wants to take off my bra, but all I want is to get him naked.

' "Help me," I beg him, and he smiles. He rips open the front of his boiler suit and peels it away from his body. He's sooo beautiful, I knew he would be. His body's perfect, like a statue in bronze or polished stone. I run my fingers over his muscles, I can't believe they're real. I don't look down. I don't want to spoil the moment. I want to enjoy the waiting . . .

'But he wants me. He's hungry. He takes my face in his hands and kisses my eyelids, my nose, my lips, my throat. Then he tilts it downwards and makes me look.

' "I want you," he says. "I want your lips round my dick." '

'He excites me so much, I just fall to my knees and tear down his briefs with my teeth. He's unbelievable . . .'

'He's big?' murmured Gabriel, nuzzling into the back of Venetia's neck as he moved, very slowly, inside her.

'Mmm, yes. Huge . . . incredible. And I want so much to touch it and taste it.'

'My mouth waters for him, my nipples ache, my clitoris is swelling and I'm rubbing my thighs together, desperate to bring myself off. I open my mouth. He pushes forward a little, and I panic. What if it won't fit inside? I resist, but he takes me ever so gently and whispers to me: "Go on, it's all right. Trust me." Slowly I open my mouth and his cock-tip slides into me. Oh, but it tastes like heaven. So strong, so masculine, the taste and the texture and the odour of raw sex.

'He's eager, I can feel him trembling, only just managing to hold back. But I don't wait for him to take me. I take him. I open my mouth as wide as it

112

will go, and I swallow him up, impaling myself on the beautiful spike of his manhood.

'For a few seconds I panic. I think I'm going to gag, throw up, spoil everything. But it's incredible, it's so perfect. He slides further and further into me, he's pushing against the back of my throat, he's in me into the hilt and I'm cradling his balls and they're so heavy and full of juice. I'm kneeling in a pool of filthy engine oil, but I don't care. All I can think about is pleasure . . .'

Gabriel listened to her, his heart thumping, the temperature rising. It required a superhuman effort not to come, and he could feel Venetia shaking, tense with the expectancy of orgasm. But he wanted to hold her there, keep them both on the edge just that little longer . . .

'What now, Venetia? What are you doing?'

'I'm sucking his dick. It's getting harder, I can taste a little trickle of salty liquid on my tongue. Now he's pulling out – I don't want him to, but he's sliding out from between my lips. And now he's masturbating as I suck his balls, spurting his hot white cream all over my face . . .

'And we're falling onto the filthy floor. He's still hard. I'm lying on my side and he's facing me, pushing between my thighs, burying himself inside me. He knows how close I am to orgasm.'

She shuddered, so very close now. Longing for Gabriel to press harder on her clitoris, she ground herself against his finger. But he held back, keeping her hungry, depriving her of the last, incredible explosion.

'There's someone else now,' he breathed into her ear. 'Another man, can't you feel him?'

'Feel him . . . yes . . .'

'He's behind you. He's lying on the ground and he's caressing your backside. He wants to fuck you, Venetia. He wants to fuck you as well.'

Venetia trembled as Gabriel's fingertip pushed into her. Sweat trickled down her face; she felt weak, wondered if any moment now her strength would give out and she would disappear, splashing and gasping, beneath the fragrant bathwater.

'Gabriel. Gabriel, I can't take any more!'

'Of course you can. Can you feel him? You have two lovers now, the lover who's screwing your beautiful pussy, and the lover who's pushing hard into your backside. Doesn't it feel good to be taken by two men at once? Doesn't it . . . ?'

As Gabriel's finger slid inside her to the knuckle, Venetia yielded to the power of her need. Orgasm flashed like white lightning, the first, thunderous explosion followed by wave upon wave of pleasure.

Gabriel held her tightly as she climaxed, the pleasure of his own orgasm overshadowed by the pleasure of knowing how much sensual domination he had over this young woman who believed, so wrongly, that she did not need him.

The following evening, Venetia found herself unexpectedly alone with her thoughts. Thoughts of work, of how to find a solution to the problem of Gabriel – and thoughts of Esteban.

Since their meeting in the coffee house, Venetia had tried again and again to rid herself of his memory. She cursed him in the silence of her heart – the same heart that ached for him to return and tell her that everything had been a bad dream. And she cursed herself for not being strong enough to forget him.

And what of Gabriel Engelhart? Right now, he was far more of a problem to her than Esteban. She wondered how a man she disliked so much could have such a powerful sexual hold over her. When she was away from him, she knew exactly what she was going to say, everything that she would do to distance herself from him. But as soon as he came to her, kissed her, awoke unwilling desires within her, she became his prisoner again. It made her angry, frustrated, and just a little afraid.

She picked up Gabriel's note and read it again. It was short, but concise: *Order dinner to be brought to my suite. I will join you later. G.*

At eight-thirty, dinner arrived on a trolley, accompanied by a rather handsome young waiter in a crisp white uniform. He looked around the room, puzzled.

'Dinner for two, madam?'

'It's all right, my . . . friend will be joining me shortly.' She pressed a tip into the waiter's hand and shooed him away, grateful to be on her own again. She almost dared to hope that Gabriel's business deals might keep him out so late that she would get to spend the whole night on her own. And tonight, she would remember to lock the connecting door. Tomorrow, perhaps, she would suggest to Gabriel that it would be best for her to stay somewhere else. She didn't need this luxury. All she needed was a room to sleep and work in, a telephone, simple food . . .

And I don't need you, whispered a voice in her head. A cold finger stroked down the back of

Venetia's neck as she wondered how Gabriel would react. Maybe it would be best if she cut her losses, packed her bags one day when he was out, and headed off somewhere, anywhere, to begin all over again.

The sound of a key turning in the lock brought an end to Venetia's train of thought. She looked up to see the door swinging open, and Gabriel standing in the doorway.

He looked good, there was no denying it. His golden hair, bleached whiter by the hot sun, glistened in the soft light. His tanned skin, his regular features, his blue eyes – he was the stuff of every hot-blooded woman's dreams. But he made her uneasy, with that steady gaze, that enigmatic expression which made her wonder what new 'games' he had in store for her.

'Good day?' she asked as she spooned chilled gazpacho into a fine porcelain dish.

'Very . . . instructive.'

'Did you find out anything about the book?'

'Not as such.'

Gabriel walked round behind Venetia's chair and pushed aside her hair, baring her neck. He began stroking and massaging her shoulders. 'You look tired,' he commented. 'As if you've been overdoing things.'

Venetia shrugged. 'Oh, you know. I went to that museum on the other side of Cairo, and showed them the picture. They said they'd never heard of the *Lore of Madali*, but I'm not sure I believed them. I could have sworn there was something the curator wasn't telling me.'

'Quite.' Gabriel squeezed Venetia's shoulders so hard that she winced. 'It's so difficult to know who is telling the truth.'

She slewed her head round to look up at him. 'What do you mean?'

'Just that.' Gabriel walked round to his chair and sat down. 'What did you do?'

'I went to the museum, I told you.'

'And yesterday? What did you do yesterday afternoon?'

Venetia stiffened. 'I told you.'

'Tell me again.'

'I visited practically every antiquities dealer in Cairo.'

'And?'

Venetia hesitated for a fraction of a second. 'Nothing.'

Gabriel put down his spoon, very coldly and calmly. He looked Venetia full in the face. 'You're lying.'

'Why should I lie?'

'Because you have something to hide? Another man, perhaps? A man you met in a restaurant?'

Venetia's blood froze. Esteban. He must have seen her with Esteban. But . . . 'How the hell . . .?'

'I had you followed. You could say I'm protecting my investment.'

Incensed now, Venetia got to her feet. 'I don't have to tell you every damn thing I do and everyone I speak to.'

Gabriel ignored her attack and went on talking. 'I wouldn't have thought that loser was your type, Venetia – but then again, I've known you long enough now to know that you'll screw any man if you're hot enough. That's right, isn't it? You're just a slut at heart.'

'How dare you!' She raised her hand to slap

him across the face, but he caught it in mid air.

'Did you let him fuck you?'

Venetia glared back at Gabriel, too angry to be afraid. 'You make me sick.'

'Well, did you?'

She was almost tempted to say yes, of course she had, she was a slut wasn't she? 'Go to hell!'

This time she succeeded in freeing herself from Gabriel's grip. She backed away, but he came after her. 'You're mine, Venetia. Mine. I paid for you to come here, I even paid for the dress you're wearing. You *owe* me.'

They struggled, Gabriel trying to force his lips against hers. When her eyes met Gabriel's, a peculiar, hypnotic warmth made Venetia's head swim, taking the edge off her anger, making her feel . . . sexy. Surprisingly sexy.

'I've got to have you, Venetia. Got to have you.'

'No. No, Gabriel.'

'Don't betray me. You've no right to betray me, it makes no sense, you want me, not some other man . . .'

She forced herself to look away, not to meet his gaze. He seized her by the hair and twisted it into an imprisoning rope, but as he pulled her head round, she spat in his face.

A white blob of spittle hit him on the cheek, and trickled slowly down the side of his face. As though shocked into a realisation of what he was doing, Gabriel let go of her and stood stock-still, the colour draining from his face. His lips moved, forming soundless words.

Venetia backed away, never taking her eyes off Gabriel, certain that he would make some move to drag her back. 'Don't you dare touch me, ever again,' she whispered hoarsely. 'If you lay one finger on me . . .'

Gabriel took one step forward. Venetia could not read his expression. It seemed to be caught between shock, anger and fear.

'But Venetia . . .' he began, very quietly, very calmly, reaching out his hand.

But Venetia shook her head. 'No more buts,' she replied. 'Just keep your hands off me, understand?'

And slamming the interconnecting door behind her, she locked it and threw the key onto the bed.

Chapter Seven

THE NILE CRUISER slid slowly upstream. From the banks on either side, peasant children watched amid the ruins of ancient tombs and temples.

But Venetia paid them little heed. Sitting in the saloon, she toyed half-heartedly with a gin and tonic, rolling the glass between her fingers as she pondered the mess she had made of everything.

The first mistake had been in letting Marcus Hale persuade her to have anything to do with Gabriel Engelhart. The second – and it was a big one – had been to get involved with Gabriel. What had she been thinking of? Why hadn't she just stayed on in Malta, enjoying Demetrios's uncomplicated company until the project finally ran out of money and she moved on to another job?

She took a sip of her drink. Of course, the third mistake had been to expect Gabriel to behave like a normal human being. She should have guessed that someone as obsessive as Engelhart would 'keep an eye on' her. Still, at least she had got away from him, if only for a few days; a breathing space to sort herself out.

Pushing her empty glass across the bar, she called out, 'Same again, please.'

'Certainly, madam.' The barman peered at her as he cut a thin sliver from a fresh lemon. 'You are not going ashore with the others? It is a beautiful day.'

'It sure is, honey,' cut in a rotund American matron in loud check trousers and a sun-hat. 'Say, why don't you come along with Eddie and me? We're gonna take a ride on a camel.'

Venetia couldn't suppress a smile of sympathy for the camel. 'Thank you, you're very kind, but no. I think I'll just stay here and laze about.'

Taking her drink, Venetia walked across to the window and sat down. A moment later, she became aware of someone sitting down next to her. She ignored the presence until a familiar voice cut into her thoughts.

'I warned you about him, Venetia. Gabriel Engelhart is a dangerous man. A man without honour.'

Shocked, she turned to see Esteban sitting beside her, a glass of red wine in his hand, his eyes enigmatic behind mirror shades.

'What the hell . . .?'

'Did I shock you? That was not my intention.' Esteban sipped his wine and grimaced. 'A very poor vintage. Not even adequate for American tourists.'

'How did you get here?'

'That is not important.'

'I told you not to follow me.'

'And what if I said I simply happened to be in the same place at the same time?'

121

'Then I'd say you were lying. So why don't you just get on with it, and tell me what you're doing here?'

'Let us just say that someone has to ensure you do not get yourself into any more trouble.'

'I told you, Esteban, I don't need this! I don't need anybody's help, and especially not yours.'

Esteban seemed perfectly unruffled. He looked immaculate as ever, thought Venetia; dressed in a loose-fitting shirt of fine white lawn and skintight black leather trousers that clung to his hips and thighs.

'How long has it been since I last saw you, *petite anglaise*? A year? Two?'

'Almost two, for what it's worth.'

Don't make me think about it, please, please, don't make me, Venetia begged silently. But it was too late. All the old feelings were flooding through her, the memories of passion and danger crowding out every other thought in her head.

'Time is a difficult concept for me,' commented Esteban. 'Days and nights . . . each one is but the tiniest stitch in the fabric of eternity.' He turned to look at her, but he did not take off his glasses. Venetia found herself wondering if his eyes betrayed more emotion than his handsome yet impassive face. 'For me, as you know, eternity is a reality. I cannot escape it.'

'Why have you followed me here?' repeated Venetia.

'To speak with you.' He paused. 'And then I will never contact you again, if that is your wish. You have my word.'

Venetia did not reply. She could not. How could she speak without betraying the tumult of conflicting emotions within her? Esteban moved closer, laying his hand lightly upon hers. It felt cool as marble, yet its touch burned like a steady flame.

'We had a bargain once. I agreed to help you to rescue your sister, and in return . . .'

Fear flashed through Venetia. She drew her hand sharply away. 'You freed me from that bargain, Esteban. The debt is paid. I owe you nothing.'

He nodded. 'I do not deny it. But you feel no regret?'

His voice was soft and warm, gentle as the breeze wafting across the river. She felt uncertain, confused, afraid of the emotions which would not go away.

'Regret?' She tried to sound incredulous. 'You gave me back my life, Esteban. Why would I regret that?'

'But immortality, Venetia. Think of it. Never to die . . .'

She looked across at him and, very deliberately, reached up and took off his sunglasses. He flinched slightly in the bright sunshine, his sensitivity to light the only outward sign that Esteban was not as other men.

'Look at me, Esteban. Look me in the eyes and tell me that you do not regret what you are. Look at me, and swear that what you suffer is not a curse.'

He did not look away, but Venetia saw the shadow of a very old, very deep wound pass across his eyes.

'Eternity is a long time. And a man may regret many things if he is alone.'

Their fingers met. The touch brought everything back; and for the first time in two years, Venetia admitted to herself what she had never admitted to Esteban. That she loved him. Loved with a raw, violent, enduring passion which reached out to him in spite of her determination to reject him. That she had loved him almost to the damnation of her eternal soul . . .

Esteban's lips brushed her cheek, her closed eyes, her lips; then darted kisses down her throat. Venetia felt the pain of longing, a burning ache in her belly. But as his kiss lingered on her throat a moment too long, she drew away.

'There can never be anything between us, Esteban. It was you who said so, don't you remember? That first night . . .'

That was before I lost my reason, thought Esteban. Before I met you, *petite anglaise*, before you came and showed me not what I am, but what I might have been. With deep regret, he lifted Venetia's hand to his lips, kissed it and let it go.

'What if I was not as I am now?' he said quietly.

'I don't understand.'

'What if I was as other men? Mortal, as you are?'

'That's crazy, Esteban. It's impossible, you know it is.' She turned away. 'No, never. There could never be any hope for us.'

Esteban infuriated her by smiling. 'So headstrong, *petite anglaise*. Always so very sure that you are right.'

Petite anglaise. Only Esteban had ever called her that. Had ever *dared* call her that. She felt the tiny hairs on the back of her neck bristle, making the

124

skin tingle. 'There's no point in this, Esteban. What are you trying to do? Torment me? Drive me crazy?'

'On the contrary, Venetia. I am trying to open your mind to reality. No, not that. To possibilities.'

She looked at him sharply. 'Is this some kind of joke?'

'You should know me better than that by now.' Esteban held his wine glass up to the light. The red liquid within seemed to swirl and glow with an inner life, tantalisingly deep and distant. He snapped his fingers, and the red wine turned a pale, lustrous yellow. 'Things are not always as they seem, *petite anglaise*.'

'Don't try to trick me, Esteban. I won't let you hurt me, not again.'

'Open your mind, Venetia. That is all I ask.'

Venetia turned away, irritated and confused. Why did Esteban have to talk in riddles? Come to that, why did he have to be here at all? She turned back to tell him what she really felt: that she didn't need this, that above all she didn't need *him*.

'Esteban, you . . .'

Her voice petered out. Esteban was gone. His chair was empty, but on the seat lay something Venetia had seen before. A book, heavy and leather-bound, bearing the symbol of a golden star within a circle, embossed in the top right-hand corner.

The barman called to her across the room.

'Your friend had gone, madam? I did not see him go.'

'I . . . no.' Venetia pushed her glass across the bar counter. 'Give me another. A double.'

As the barman poured the drink, Venetia

125

reached out and stroked the leather binding of the old book. It was the one she and Esteban had almost come to blows over in the restaurant. The one she had been only too glad to let him have, once she'd realised that it wasn't the *Lore of Madali*. But what could it possibly contain that would be of interest to Esteban? He'd said himself that it wasn't the medieval grimoire he had been looking for, just some tedious old diary. And why had he brought it here. . .?'

'Your drink, madam.'

She took a sip of the cold liquid. It tasted fruity, a little acid, the iciness searing her throat as she swallowed.

Opening the book, she saw an embroidered silk ribbon marking a page. She flipped through the dusty, yellowed leaves until she reached the place. It was just another diary entry. Just another boring day in some uninteresting person's forgotten life. But there was also a note in Esteban's hand, attached to the silk bookmark:

'Read and understand, *petite anglaise*. Read and believe that all things may be possible. Esteban.'

'Rien ne va plus.'

The croupier called in the stakes, and a dozen pairs of eyes watched the roulette wheel spin, laden with their hopes and fears. Fortunes were won and lost every night in the casino at the Hotel Oasis, absolutely the most exclusive gambling club in the Nile delta.

The hotel had been built in the mid-nineteenth century, in the days of colonialism and patronage; and it still retained a certain crumbling grandeur, a golden decadence enhanced by the individualism of its patrons. Professional gamblers mingled with aristocrats, rogues and chancers, nameless adventurers passing through, never to be seen here again.

Esteban was at home here. In the centuries since vampirism had cursed him to eternal life, he had found ways and means of getting by. He lived quietly in his villa above Valazur, spending his nights in the casinos and gambling clubs, earning a good living and relieving the boredom of immortality. No one asked questions about the dark-haired, olive-skinned stranger who lived on the hill above the sea. No one questioned that a man might live from decade to decade and never change, never age. No one questioned him because he had taught them well. He had taught them to fear him.

The man to his right at the poker table – a fat Lebanese with as many gold rings as he had fingers – slapped a wad of notes down on the table, taking a self-satisfied pull on his cigar.

'Fifty.'

Esteban peeled ten notes from the roll at his side and laid them neatly on the table, pushing them towards the centre.

'I'll raise you five hundred.'

A ripple of interest ran round the table. Faces searched his, certain that they could read a clue there. Was he bluffing? Esteban's expression remained enigmatic, unfathomable. He was an excellent poker player. But then again, he had had seven hundred years in which to perfect the art.

He glanced down at the cards in his hand. The Queen of Hearts. Of course; it was as he had thought. This time he allowed himself a smile, laying down the royal flush and raking in his winnings. 'If you gentlemen will excuse me for a moment.'

A hand touched his arm, and a gruff voice interjected, 'Nobody leaves this table until I'm good and ready.'

Esteban fixed the Lebanese with a cold-eyed stare. 'Take your hands off me.'

'Sit down and play the game.'

Esteban let out an impatient sigh. He had been aware all along of the knife concealed in the man's sleeve, but had hoped to avoid this unpleasantness. The blade glinted in the Lebanese's hand. With a single, swift movement Esteban seized the knife by the blade and twisted it out of his fingers. The Lebanese winced, partly in pain, partly in astonishment that this tall, rangy loner could carry such strength in his spare frame. His eyes widened as Esteban wiped his bloody fingers on a napkin. Seconds later, the thin knife-cut had healed without trace.

Pocketing his winnings, Esteban crossed the salon and walked out into the main foyer. He felt for the card in his pocket, and walked on.

She was there, as he had known she would be, more beautiful even than he had remembered her. Her tall, slender frame was flattered by the ice-blue sheath dress, with its froth of pale silk swishing behind her on the polished parquet floor and its low-cut, décolleté bodice. A diamanté necklace sparkled at her throat, a single ruby-red drop caressing the soft valley between her breasts.

The Queen of Hearts.

He ran the tip of his tongue across his parched lips.

Venetia turned and saw him. Then walked towards him, slowly, hesitantly. Esteban greeted her almost warily, nodding his acknowledgement of her presence. 'I . . . hoped you would come.'

Venetia shook her head. 'You knew I would come.'

Esteban's grey eyes met hers and a shiver of recognition passed between them. 'Yes. Yes, you are right.' He looked at Venetia and knew that she had read the diary, every word. Knew that she had understood.

'Walk with me,' said Venetia. 'There are things I need to talk to you about, things I need to ask you . . .'

Esteban shook his head.

'We will not speak of these things now. There will be a time to talk. Tonight . . .' His eyes caressed her, running over her skin, taking in every sweet curve of her body. 'Tonight I wish to know you again. To remember the smell and the taste of you.'

They walked out into the hotel gardens: a riot of half-wild flowers and trees, tumbling down to the river's edge. The air was very still, very calm, the sky vast and starry. They walked together, very close but not quite touching. It was as though there was some invisible force which both drew and repelled them; made it as impossible for them to exist together as apart.

'Gabriel Engelhart – you and he are lovers.' It was a statement, not a question.

'What business is that of yours?' Venetia's voice quavered. She could not lie to Esteban, only evade his questions.

'But you *are* lovers.'

'We were,' Venetia admitted. 'Not any more. I've left him.'

Esteban sighed.

'I warned you, *petite anglaise*. I warned you and you laughed in my face.'

She turned towards him, her face half in shadow and half in light. 'It *was* you in the dream, wasn't it?'

'Perhaps. Perhaps not.'

'There are things even you can't protect me from, Esteban. Things I have to discover for myself.'

'Even if they bring you into mortal danger?'

'What is life without danger, Esteban?'

He looked into her face and felt the huge, juggernaut force of his obsession, crushing and devouring him. Without her, time stretched before him like an empty road through a waterless desert.

'Walk with me.'

He took her arm and led her down cracked stone steps, into a secluded glade between date palms. At its centre lay an irregularly-shaped pool lined with black marble, surrounded by the broken pillars and tumbling stones of an ancient civilisation, dragged here by some well-meaning but ignorant colonial to provide 'atmosphere'. Esteban despised ignorant people – and yet hadn't he been ignorant himself, once? It was his own arrogant stupidity which had created him as he now was: a man of power, with no power over his own existence.

Stone benches were arranged about the pool.

Esteban motioned to Venetia to sit. He stood beside the water, gazing into the middle-distance, breathing in the scents and sounds of the night. His night. Letting the darkness soothe his pain.

'When you left Valazur,' he began, 'I made up my mind to despise you. I had been wrong about you. You were nothing but an empty-headed *anglaise*, just like your sister Cassie.'

'You had every right to despise me. After all, I had refused you what you wanted, and you *always* get what you want.'

He laughed, turning to look at Venetia over his shoulder. His eyes glittered in the darkness like black diamonds.

'Always so spirited, so *charmante*, so *ironique*. And you must know that I do not despise you, that I cannot despise you. That I . . .' He did not speak the word in his heart, it was not fitting. Could love exist where the heart had long since turned to hollow blackness? 'It is good to see you once more, Venetia Fellowes.'

Venetia got to her feet and walked across to join him beside the pool.

'I tried to forget you,' she whispered. 'I tried so hard. How can you come back and do this to me?'

'You are free to go, if that is what you wish. I will do nothing to hold you here.'

They stood in silence for a few moments. Venetia heard the sound of her own heart thumping in the silence, certain that Esteban must be able to hear it too, that he must feel nothing but scorn for her. And she wanted so much to hate him for forcing his way back into her life. But now, after what had happened on the Nile boat, reason seemed to have evaporated,

131

leaving only the passion. The white-hot, searing passion which drew her to him as she had never been drawn to any man. She knew the danger, she knew the impossibility; but Esteban was like an addiction. How could she live without him, now that he had found her once again?

'But you know that I will stay. Why are you always right, Esteban?' she demanded, half-bitterly, half in humour.

'Not always. I thought you would stay with me before, remember that. I was so sure you could not resist me.'

Esteban plucked a flower and cast it onto the dark, shimmering surface of the pool. It bobbed on the surface for a few moments, swirling on the undercurrents like a whirling dancer; then was drawn into the depths and lost.

'You read the marked passages in the diary.'

'Yes.'

'Then you know that what I crave is not impossible.' He reached out and took Venetia by the wrists. His grip was vice-tight.

'You're hurting me, Esteban.'

He seemed not to notice. He was lost in her eyes, lost in his own words.

'It is *not impossible*. Do you know what that means?'

'But Esteban, you're talking about an old diary, we don't know that it's true, we don't even know if the book is authentic . . .' Venetia didn't even believe herself. She knew that Esteban could hear the excitement in her voice, knew that she dared to hope, as he did. 'Let's face it, we don't even know if Marcus Almenius existed, let alone whether this is really the diary of his travels.'

'If I were not a vampire . . .'

'Don't say it, Esteban.'

'If this curse could be torn from me, Venetia . . . I would endure any pain, any torment . . .'

No other words passed between them. Words could not express the feelings which surged through their bodies, the hunger which could only be expressed through touch, and kiss, and caress.

Esteban took Venetia in his arms, lifting her up as though she were light as a feather, holding her aloft so that she seemed to fly above him like a pale blue angel, her dress falling in soft folds about him. For a fleeting moment they were no longer joined to the earth. They were incorporeal beings, supernatural spirits tumbling and soaring in the warm darkness of the starry sky, free and powerful and unfettered.

Pulling her down towards him, Esteban crushed his lips against hers. Venetia met his kiss hungrily, her belly filled by a ravenous need to join her body to Esteban's. She knew it was crazy, knew it might even be a trick. One kiss at her throat – one small bite from those sharp teeth; the warm wetness of fresh blood, and she would be his for ever, lured into immortality as a moth is lured into the fatal brightness of the candle flame.

But in these blissful moments, Venetia cared nothing for danger. She pressed her mouth against Esteban's, tasting the coolness of his saliva mingling with hers, her tongue and his jousting, thrusting, intertwining as their bodies remembered and explored and exulted.

Leading Venetia by the hand, Esteban walked slowly down the steps which led into the pool.

The water was only waist-deep, but its coolness made Venetia shiver deliciously as it lapped about her ankles, her calves, her thighs. For a fleeting instant she thought of her dress – her one, good evening dress – it would be ruined. Then the thought faded away into insignificance. All that mattered, all that existed in the here and now, was the desire.

'Trust me.'

Esteban's words sounded in her head like the shimmer of a cymbal, a spreading vibration, echoing again and again.

One hand was behind her head, tilting it back so that he could plant more and still more kisses on her willing mouth; the other was sliding down the zipper at the back of her evening gown.

She wriggled her spine to help him, and the zipper glided down with a soft sigh, baring her back to the soft night air.

Her fingers reached out, smoothing down Esteban's back. His long, thigh-length black jacket was cut tightly to the contours of his tall, slim, almost rangy body. She felt the hardness of muscle. He wriggled out of his jacket and it slipped from him into the water, floating on the surface like a black shadow.

Underneath, Esteban was wearing a loose-fitting evening shirt, the cool, crisp cotton slightly moist with sweat. Venetia's fingers ruched up the back of his shirt, hungry for him. Despite the heat of the day his flesh felt cool and smooth.

Esteban peeled away the bodice of Venetia's evening dress and its own heaviness sent it slithering softly down her body, into the water beneath. She heard herself giggle with exhilaration, stepping out of the dress and standing before her lover in strapless ivory basque and stockings, framing tiny lace briefs which offered tantalising glimpses of golden-blonde curls.

Esteban did not unfasten the hooks at the back of Venetia's basque. Instead, he slid his hands into the cups and cradled her breasts with a sensual tenderness. She moaned softly as he stroked the flat of his thumb across her nipple, making it pout and blush with sheer pleasure.

There was a familiar sensation of wetness between Venetia's thighs. She rubbed them together, delighting in the excitement, each soft frou-frou of stockinged thigh making the hood of her clitoris slide gently back and forth, driving her to new peaks of excitement.

Her fingers fumbled with Esteban's shirt. Hunger was taking over now, making her reckless and crazy. What did she care if anyone took a walk through the hotel gardens and found them here, making uninhibited love in the middle of the ornamental pond? What did she care about anything, except having Esteban's kisses on her breasts, and his fingers so, so tenderly sliding down her panties over her willing hips?

Esteban's belt yielded easily and she unbuttoned his flies, her fingers remembering the first blissful time she had touched him. She yearned to touch and kiss him again, to rediscover the beauty of his manhood.

'Venetia. *Petite anglaise . . . Ah, que tu as le diable dans les doigts. Touche-moi, touche-moi, baise-moi avec tes doigts de feu . . .'*

Esteban closed his eyes and explored Venetia by touch alone, his whole body singing with ecstasy at the touch of her fingers on his naked penis.

Venetia sank to her knees in the water, its coldness making the breath shudder from her. Her hair floated out behind her in wet rat's-tails, but she paid it no heed. All she saw, all she cared about, was the beautiful lance of flesh cradled in her hands.

He was more beautiful even than she remembered. His penis was hard and smooth as carved stone, a marbled sabre that curved and swelled to a bulbous plum of a glans, pierced through with a ring of polished haematite. Venetia put out her tongue and tasted it, rolling it round in her mouth, sucking and biting.

Esteban cursed softly under his breath, his grip tightening on her breasts, squeezing and pinching the nipples.

'Nom de diable . . .'

He let out a long, low growl as Venetia took his penis into her mouth, swallowing it down with a sweet, savage reverence. Her fingers squeezed and stroked his balls, so overfull with their tribute to her loveliness that he almost spurted into her at her first touch.

With long, smooth strokes, Venetia sucked him, her lips tightening joyfully about the ramrod of his manhood. She knew that he was close to orgasm; knew that she had only to tease the stone cock-ring a little more and he would offer up the creamy bounty of his tribute, filling her mouth and throat so full that his seed would spill from between her lips, trickling down over chin and throat.

To her surprise, he withdrew from her

suddenly, gently but firmly pushing her away.
She heard him panting hoarsely in the darkness.

'Not yet,' he whispered. 'I desire you, *petite
anglaise*. Let me show you how I desire you.'

Tightly clasped in each other's arms, they sank
together into the water. It rose up Venetia's body,
lapping at her face, and she began to struggle,
panicking.

'Esteban . . . Esteban . . .'

'Do not be afraid. You must not fear me, you
must trust me. With trust, all things can be made
possible . . .'

His words soothed her, and it seemed to
Venetia that she was floating in some trance-like
realm where nothing existed but the joining of
her body to Esteban's; the white-hot searing of
pleasure as he slid between her thighs, possess-
ing her body and soul.

The waters washed over them again and again
as they fucked, their bodies rolling and tumbling
together; one unity of pleasure. She could not
breathe; but she did not need to breathe. She
could not speak; but words were superfluous.

For endless, precious moments, until the pure
white light of orgasm summoned her back to
reality, Venetia understood what it could mean to
feel a passion that transcended everything.

Even the boundaries between life and death.

Chapter Eight

AS THE TAXI wove its way through the crowded
streets and headed out towards the airport,
Venetia took a brief look back over her shoulder.

Somewhere back there, in the teeming mass
that was Cairo, Gabriel Engelhart was waiting for
her to turn up and explain herself. And what was
the betting that he was not pleased – not pleased
at all?

Esteban was sitting beside her, engimatic once
more behind the dark glasses which protected his
sensitive eyes from the full glare of the sun.

'You are unsure about this?' he asked her. 'You
wish to return?'

Venetia shook her head. 'I'm perfectly sure.'
She paused. 'I'm just worried about Gabriel.
About what he'll do when he realises I really have
left him . . .'

'You don't owe him anything.'

'No, but . . .'

'And he doesn't own you.' Esteban leant
towards her. 'Or does he?'

'No!' Venetia shook that thought right out of

her head. 'Nobody owns me.' Including you Esteban, she thought to herself as she looked at him, loving and hating and desiring him all at once. 'I chickened out and posted him a letter,' she explained. 'He should get it tomorrow or the next day.'

'Then that is settled.'

'Where do we go next?'

'We will take a plane to Halab in Syria, then we must travel across the desert to the oasis spoken of in the book. When we reach the mountains, we must find a guide.'

Esteban sat back in his seat. He seemed edgy to Venetia.

'Esteban . . .'

'Mmm?'

'There's something wrong, isn't there?'

Esteban gave a dry laugh. 'I always did admire your skill with the understatement, Venetia Fellowes.' His long, slender fingers fiddled with the strap of his Cartier watch. 'If I could only be certain . . .'

Venetia knew what Esteban was thinking about. She hadn't been able to get it out of her mind ever since she had read the extract from the diary they had found in the restaurant.

Despite the star and circle embossed on the binding, the book had turned out to be the diary of a man called Marcus Almenius, a medieval alchemist who had travelled widely in the Middle East. Nothing so very remarkable about that, perhaps – except for the section which had related his discovery of a settlement, high in the mountains, cut off for many years from the outside world.

Almenius related the story of how he arrived, half-starved and delirius with fever, at a town hewn from the mountainside. The inhabitants had taken him in and nursed him back to health; and over the weeks he spent with them, Almenius had begun to learn some of their most esoteric mysteries.

'Do you think . . .?' began Venetia.

'Do I think what?'

'Do you think the settlement still exists?'

Esteban shrugged. He gazed out of the taxi window at the dusty scrubland beyond the city. 'Who can tell?'

'I can't imagine that we'll ever be able to find it, even if we follow Almenius's directions. They're so vague. And do you really believe that these people have the power . . .?'

'That they could "cure" vampires? Remove the curse from them and restore them to life?' Esteban's whole body seemed to tense. 'You are right, Venetia. In the cold light of day it seems ridiculous. Perhaps we should turn back now.'

'No.' Venetia ran her hands over the age-smoothed leather binding of Marcus Almenius's journal.

'There could be danger ahead. Grave danger. God knows, Venetia, there is danger for you even in being with me . . .'

Esteban shuddered inwardly as, deep in the recesses of his soul, there stirred the ancient, dark hunger. For as long as that hunger endured, he could never quite trust himself, knowing how many had perished to satisfy the desire which could be suppressed but never killed. The true curse of his vampirism, the true horror and punishment, lay in the fact that he loathed himself for what he had become.

'You would never hurt me.'

He shook his head slowly.

'Not willingly, that is true. But you cannot understand the darkness that overtakes me. I fear for you Venetia. As long as you are by my side, I fear for you.'

And I fear for myself, thought Venetia. But if there is even the faintest chance that Esteban can be cured, this is a risk which I must take.

The flame of need flared higher as the sun rose to its zenith in the Tunisian sky.

In the basement of his town house, Gabriel Engelhart raked his fingernails down the blonde girl's back. She arched her spine and gave a little soft hiss, unable to resist or free herself from the leather straps which bound her wrists and ankles. Gabriel smiled grimly at the sight of the white scratches, turning to raised pink welts before his eyes.

'This girl's skin is particularly sensitive,' he commented.

Ismail permitted himself a self-satisfied nod.

'I picked her out for you myself, master, on my last trip to Sweden. Her name is Jutta. I knew that she would please you.'

Gabriel gave the girl's rump a hard slap. It jumped up, quivering and reddening at the blow.

'You say she is still a virgin? I find that hard to believe.'

'It is indeed rare for a Scandinavian girl, master. But this one was taken from a convent school.' His thin, cracked lips twitched in amusement.

'Her parents wished her to become a nun.'

Gabriel laughed drily. 'I can see from her hard nipples that this one is made for a very different kind of devotion. You have done your job well, Ismail. Have her and the others prepared for my pleasure.'

Ismail's raised eyebrow was the only outward sign of his surprise. 'For your own pleasure, master? I had thought this consignment were for auction . . .'

Gabriel took a silver nipple-clamp and opened its cruel, alligator jaws. It was true that he did not normally sample the merchandise himself – particularly the virgins. That only reduced their value on the open market. But today was different. Venetia Fellowes had betrayed him and his anger and hatred and frustrated lust boiled for release. Somebody was going to have to pay . . .

The sun sat low in the sky, moving swiftly now towards twilight and the sudden, starry darkness of a Syrian night.

Venetia and Esteban sat cross-legged on a hand-woven carpet, beneath a canopy of brightly-coloured rugs. A Kurdish woman in long, dark robes and a headdress decorated with silver coins moved about the tent, serving thick, bitter coffee and sticky sweetmeats. Venetia felt a pang of guilt that she should have to wait on them, but when she tried to thank her, the woman averted her gaze. Uncomfortable in her Western clothes, Venetia drew up her knees and covered them with her floaty cotton skirt.

The nomad chief nodded and drew deeply on his hookah pipe, drawing in warm tobacco smoke sweet with honey. He was an impressive man in his middle years, powerfully built with a hooked nose and a dark beard, glossy with scented oil. There was also something in his eyes – a covetousness – which Venetia found faintly alarming.

'You say you wish to cross the desert. Why is this?'

Venetia opened her mouth to speak, but Esteban threw her a look and she shut it again. It was difficult to play the game when you didn't care for the rules, she thought to herself, and she had never been one to play second fiddle to anyone.

'We wish to cross the border and travel into the mountains,' replied Esteban.

'You are Westerners. You have visas?'

'No.'

'Crossing the border is forbidden for you without visas.'

'We know.'

The chief's eyes twinkled with quiet humour. 'There are other ways of reaching Iraq. By aeroplane. By railway, even . . .'

'Not where we wish to go,' cut in Venetia, not speaking in English but in the tribe's own dialect. The chief raised an eyebrow, clearly impressed by Venetia's knowledge of his language, but not accustomed to being addressed so directly by a woman.

'Women should learn to speak when they are spoken to,' observed the chief, more in amusement than anger. 'Lest their foolish chatter sound like the bleating of goats.'

With difficulty, Venetia controlled the urge to

tell him to mind his manners. She could see Esteban watching her out of the corner of her eye.

'I beg your pardon my lord,' she said. 'I did not mean to speak out of turn. But my companion and I . . . we are desperate to find the settlement of which he has spoken. We need your help.'

'And what help may we offer?'

'Your wives tell me that you and your people are soon to travel across country to the mountains.'

The chief nodded. 'This is true. We are taking my daughter to her bridegroom's village. There will be a wedding, many guests. But of what interest is this to you?'

'Would you allow us to travel with you?'

'The life is hard. And your hands are soft, a lady's hands.'

'We are ready for any hardship.'

'We share all tasks and all possessions.' His eyes met Venetia's. 'Everything. Our women also. You understand?'

Venetia looked towards Esteban. Obviously he was calm, cold even; but she could feel the anger and jealousy within him. She turned away, looking the chief straight in the eyes.

'I understand.' Her mouth was dry. 'I am willing to share . . . everything.'

The Kurdish chief's expression did not change. 'Good,' he said abruptly. 'Then you and your companion may join us on our journey. We will take you as far as the foothills. And you, my dear . . . tomorrow night you shall share my tent.'

It was dark now, the night pitch-black and cold over the watering-place. Somewhere in the distance horses and camels shuffled and grunted in the blackness.

'Something is making them uneasy,' whispered Venetia, drawing very close to Esteban as they sat beside the lake. Esteban's hand tightened about hers.

'You do not have to do this,' he told her.

'You know I do,' she replied gently, almost frightened by the intensity of Esteban's kiss. 'I must spend one night with him or he will not allow us to join their caravan.'

'We will find the lost village without their help.'

'No, Esteban, the directions in the diary are too imprecise. These people know the desert and the mountains. This is the only way, you know it is true.'

'Do you desire this man?' Esteban's voice was studiedly devoid of emotion.

'No.'

'Don't lie to me, Venetia.'

'Why should I lie?' She wrapped her arms close about him, and they lay down together on the dusty earth, still warm from the heat of the sun. Esteban lay half on top of her, his thigh across hers, his hand easing open the top button of her blouse. He kissed the base of her breasts, his lips cool on her overheated flesh. Somewhere at the edge of his consciousness, a darkness was lapping like brackish water.

'If we fail . . .' he murmured.

'We will not.'

'If we fail . . . you must leave me. This must be as if it had never existed.'

'I know.' The thought entered Venetia's mind but she killed it ruthlessly. She could not afford even to think of failure.

'If I were a better man, I would make you leave me now. I would never have brought you here . . .' Esteban's hand caressed her bare belly, sliding upwards to slip underneath the bottom of her bra. 'You are my weakness Venetia, my obsession . . .' But I will not allow myself to be your destruction, he told himself in the silence of his thoughts.

Venetia drew him down on top of her and his fingers sought out her left breast, freeing it from her bra, letting his tongue flick lightly across its erect crest.

'Make love to me, Esteban,' she whispered as he took her nipple into his mouth and slid up the floaty layers of her skirt. 'Make love to me and make me forget tomorrow.'

Chapter Nine

THE WHITE ARAB stallion half-trotted, half-slithered down the sandy side of the dune. The rider shaded his eyes with his hand, surveying the horizon, then dug his heels into the horse's flanks, spurring it on. A palomino pony trotted behind, its rider leading a mule laden with pots, pans and provisions.

Before them lay the Kurdish settlement, a jumble of palm trees, colourful tents and mud-brick houses dotted around a watering-place. Camels bellowed bad-temperedly as their owner roped them together and loaded them up with baskets of dates and bundles of brightly-coloured fabric. Somewhere in the distance, a young woman was coming back from the spring, balancing a huge earthenware water pot on her head. A woman whose elegant, swaying walk reminded him in some subtle, crazy way of Venetia Fellowes . . .

As he dismounted and handed the reins of his horse to a small boy, Gabriel Engelhart wondered what madness had driven him to this. But his heart thumped with the thought that she might be here, in this place . . . with what she and her lover had stolen from him.

Ismail dismounted and followed in Gabriel's wake. 'Master.'

Gabriel turned and threw Ismail and impatient look.

'What now?'

'If we find the girl, will we take her back with us?'

'Perhaps.'

'We could sell her.' Ismail licked his lips. 'Once she has been cured of her disobedience, she would fetch a good price.'

'I have not yet decided.' At any rate, Gabriel hadn't decided quite where to begin in her long and well-deserved punishment.

'And the book, master? The *Lore of Madali*? The Englishwoman has it with her?'

'I am certain of it. Assuming she has not given it to *him*.' Her lover, thought Gabriel. Esteban, Venetia's lover. It left a bitter taste of bile in his mouth.

'The air steward was very sure that they were travelling together,' Ismail continued helpfully. 'He said there was much kissing, it was very . . . sexual . . .'

'Shut up, Ismail.' Gabriel's eyes glittered.

'Yes, master.'

'We will find them together, and we will find ways of punishing them both.'

Gabriel walked on towards the centre of the encampment. At that moment, a young boy on a motorbike came roaring out from beneath the trees, kicking up a choking cloud of sand. He thrust his hand into his pocket and held it out, the palm filled with the glitter of coloured stones.

'Very nice jewellery, very real. Buy it for your girlfriends, yes?'

'Go away.' Gabriel turned aside, but the youth followed, riding alongside at walking pace.

'You want girl, nice girl?'

Gabriel stopped and turned to look at the youth. Perhaps, just perhaps, he might prove useful.

'I am looking for someone,' he said. 'Two people, a man and a woman.'

The youth shrugged. 'I see nothing, I not know.'

Gabriel held out a small-denomination banknote. 'The man is a Spaniard – he has sallow skin and dark hair, and a face like an eagle. The woman . . .' Gabriel searched for the right words to describe Venetia Fellowes. 'The woman is English. She had golden hair and eyes that are blue like the summer sky . . .'

The Arab youth whistled. 'She beautiful, yes? She your woman who run away with another man?'

Bristling with vicarious indignation, Ismail raised his hand to strike the boy, but Gabriel shook his head. He added a second banknote to the one in his hand. 'You have seen them?'

'I not sure.'

'If you tell me where they are, I will give you money.'

The youth grinned, seizing the banknotes and pushing them into the pocket of his jeans. 'I see them. But they not here now.'

'Then where are they?'

'I take you to my sister.' The boy drew a perfect hour-glass figure in the air. 'She very beautiful. She make you welcome, drink tea with you. Perhaps she tell you what you want to know.'

Ismail caught Gabriel's arm. 'Master, it may be a trick, some deception the bitch has laid to trap us.'

With a look of contempt, Gabriel shook him free, patting the creases out of his shirt sleeve. 'Do you seriously believe the girl has the wit to deceive me?'

'And Esteban, master?'

Gabriel sneered and spat into the dust at his feet. 'You will speak no more of that filth.'

Suitably chastened, Ismail trailed his master across the settlement, following the boy with the motorbike. He felt uneasy, as though they were being watched. And in truth he could not understand why Gabriel should trouble himself about a girl and a book. Gabriel Engelhart had more books and more beautiful women than any man could ever want.

And then there was this inexplicable hatred of the man Esteban. Ismail had never met Esteban, but he knew that there was bad blood between him and his master – an animosity stretching back to the time before Ismail had come into Gabriel's service. Perhaps that was it then; a case of simple rivalry . . .

The youth led them to a low, square building of mud bricks, surrounded by gently swaying palms. A beaded curtain hung over the open doorway, and soft music floated out, shimmering on the heat haze of a desert noon.

'My sister very nice girl, very pretty.' The youth grinned and held out his palm. 'Very generous.'

150

Gabriel ignored his hopeful look and pushed him aside. 'Later. If she tells us what we want to know.'

Ismail ducked in front of him. 'Let me go first, master, in case it is a trap.'

'Don't be ridiculous. Stand aside.'

Ismail watched with the pain of frustrated self-sacrifice as his master stepped inside the house. It was his special, personal torment that Gabriel would never appreciate the lengths to which his manservant would go to prove his complete devotion.

Gabriel entered the house. It was initially dark, and he blinked to accustom his sight to the half-light. There was a strong scent of sweet spice on the air – cinnamon and something else he didn't quite recognise. From somewhere quite close by, a woman's voice whispered to him.

'Welcome. Enter. Do not be afraid.'

Afraid! If she had known Gabriel Engelhart, she would have understood that it was she who ought to feel fear.

The twilight resolved itself into light and shade, candle-flames dancing in a fuzzy halo about a dark shape.

The woman got to her feet. She was exotic, dark-skinned with thick black kohl outlining large and lustrous eyes. Tribal tattoos traced fine patterns over her forehead and cheeks, and ornate silver jewellery jingled in her pierced nose, ears and lips. She held out a brass goblet, filled with some cool, sticky-sweet liquid.

'You drink with me, stranger?'

Gabriel raised his hand and dashed the goblet from her hand. It fell to the ground, spilling its contents in a dark stain across the hem of her robe and the embroidered cushions at her feet.

'Please, no . . .' She backed away, but he did not give her the opportunity to escape from him. He seized the long, braided rope of her hair and twisted it back, forcing her to her knees before him.

'Now,' he smiled, the candlelight illuminating a spark of satisfaction in his cold blue eyes. 'Tell me about Esteban and his English bitch. And be sure you tell me *everything* you know.'

The wedding procession moved slowly across the desert and into the mountains, resting during the hottest part of the day and moving on when the sun sank low in the sky.

Venetia was well-nigh unrecognisable under the heavy, ankle-length robes she had been given to wear. At first she had protested against this badge of anonymity – until she realised that their value was as much practical as cosmetic. The long veils of black, filmy fabric protected her fair skin from the searing glare of the noonday sun. Naked underneath, she felt curiously sensual as a hot, dry wind blew the fabric against her bare limbs, soft as a lover's caress.

Adventures were all very well, thought Venetia – but right now, she was pining for a hot bath and a five-star hotel. She walked barefoot on the stony earth, obliged to walk with the other women while the menfolk rode on ponies and camels. She felt a twinge of sympathy for the chief's fourteen-year-old daughter, being carried half across the country to be delivered into the arms of a fifteen-year-old bridegroom she had never even met.

Glancing to her right, she saw Esteban. He had dismounted from his horse and was leading it into the whipping, sandy wind, his dark hair blowing out behind him and his clothes moulding themselves closely to the contours of his spare yet strong figure.

He seemed to sense her looking at him and turned to meet her gaze. There was something in his eyes, something dark and fiery, which frightened Venetia. She had deluded herself that she knew him so well, and yet there was so much in him that she had not even begun to understand. Was she wrong to trust him?

She moved towards him, but he shook his head, gesturing to her to keep her distance. Then he turned away and marched on, staring fixedly towards the horizon, his dark eyes screwed up against the pain of the sunlight. Whatever private demon was tormenting Esteban, she could do nothing to still the pain.

At a village in the foothills, they parted company with the wedding caravan. Venetia was not sorry to bid farewell to the Kurdish chief. Although he had not been unkind to her, she had loathed his touch on her naked skin, knew how much he craved for her to stay and become one of his concubines.

'I will leave you with A'shah.' The chief clapped his hands and a girl stepped forward. 'She will be your guide until your reach the place. You must make the rest of your journey alone.' His eyes coaxed Venetia to change her mind, to stay, but when all was said and done he was a realist. Nor was he blind. He had seen the way the Englishwoman's blue eyes caressed the dark-haired Spaniard. 'I wish you well. Perhaps you will return to me one day.'

The wedding party continued on its way into the village, and Venetia looked to Esteban. He would not – or could not – meet her gaze, and she saw that he was staring fixedly at A'shah. He was trembling, his hands clenched so tightly into fists that his knuckles shone bone-white through the flesh. And there was a look on his face that Venetia could not fail to recognise.

The agony of hunger.

The moon was full.

It hung over the mountains like a globe of frosted glass, huge and unreal, its soft, cold light chilling the night air.

Venetia and Esteban stood with A'shah at the top of the escarpment. Unveiled now, her handsome face was tilted up towards the moon, its light sculpting the curves of chin and throat.

'One more day's travel,' she announced in her husky voice. 'That will take us to the place.'

'You will come there with us?' asked Venetia, already knowing the answer.

A'shah shook her head. 'I cannot go, I must return to my tribe. And if you are wise, you too will turn back. There are stories . . . rumours. No one ever travels to that part of the mountains. Some have tried – and never returned.'

'We must go on. We have no choice. There is something we must find.'

'Then Allah go with you and shield your footsteps.' A'shah glanced at Esteban, standing a little way away. He was white and shaking, sweat pearling his brow as though he were in the grip of some fever. 'You are ill?'

He looked at her sharply, then looked away again, as though it gave him pain to see her.

'Do not concern yourself with me. I am quite well.'

Turning on his heel he walked quickly away, heading into a narrow gulley between the rocks. Venetia called after him. 'Esteban . . .'

He hesitated, then walked on, not looking back. Venetia followed him, as much by instinct as good sense. He was walking quickly away from the encampment, deeper and deeper into the darkness and shadows, a shadow within a shadow, becoming one with the comforting blackness that surrounded him.

'Esteban, why are you running away from me?'

This time, he looked back at her. 'Go back, Venetia.'

'There's something wrong. I won't leave you.'

'You must. It is – too dangerous.' His breath came in halting spasms, each drawn in with visible pain. His face seemed paler and more gaunt, his hands claw-like, his entire body tense as a sculpture in twisted wire.

Venetia took a hesitant step closer to him. 'Tell me, Esteban. Tell me what's wrong.'

'The darkness. Can't you see? It . . . overwhelms me. The hunger. I cannot control . . .'

And now Venetia understood. She had known that this moment must surely come. The hunger had returned to Esteban . . . the thirst for blood. 'Fight it, Esteban. Fight the hunger.'

He turned tortured eyes on her. Eyes that blazed with a passion beyond love, beyond death. 'I have no wish to harm you, Venetia. But I cannot

155

protect you. It was madness to bring you here . . .'

'We had to come, you know that. It's the only chance we have.' She reached out to touch him but he shrank away, afraid of the savagery within him.

'Feed. I must feed.' A spasm of agony crossed Esteban's face and he threw back his head, letting out a long, low moan. His fingers clawed at his face, his hair, his body, as though trying to tear out and destroy the demon within him. Slowly he sank to his knees, still shaking, clawing now at the rocks around him. 'Go back. Keep away, the power is greater than my strength. I cannot control it any longer, it tears apart my very soul . . .'

For a split second Venetia caught the mad light in his eyes and almost turned and ran. But her passion for Esteban was greater than her fear. 'Give me your knife,' she said suddenly, her voice curiously matter-of-fact. He stared back at her, uncomprehending. 'Give it to me, Esteban.'

The glimmer of understanding filtered into Esteban's pain-wracked consciousness. 'No, Venetia!'

'Give it to me.' She reached down and took the hunting knife from Esteban's belt. He was too weak to resist, the dark hunger twisting and contracting his body with spasm after spasm of ravening pain. The six-inch, curving blade caught the glitter of moonlight and flashed out a danger signal. Venetia ran her finger along the edge. It was wafer-thin, and so sharp that where it had touched, a thin line of blood sprang up.

Esteban tried to look away, but he could not tear his eyes away from the sight of Venetia's blood, the fine, dark line, the plump, salty beads springing proud upon the flesh, so alluring with their seductive, coppery scent. Drawing him, drawing him, daring him to do what he despised, and what his cursed heart screamed for him to do . . .

Taking a deep breath, Venetia drew the hunting knife very quickly across the inside of her forearm. It was all done so quickly, and the blade was so sharp, that she scarcely felt any pain.

And now the blood welled up from the cut vein in a dark crimson abundance, oozing and dripping.

'Drink, Esteban,' she whispered. And she reached out to him. 'Drink . . .'

A cry of release escaped from Esteban as he caught the first, fat droplet between his parted lips. For him, this was the elixir of life – of his cursed, unending servitude. Of his passion which could never end.

He drank deeply, his tongue lapping like a cat's at Venetia's blood, his lips sucking, catching every last droplet. It was a small gift, scarcely enough to still the dark hunger; but it freed him from the agony of urgent need. Slowly his muscles began to relax, the pounding in his head stilled by the deep, ecstatic warmth which stole over him, filling him with a very different desire.

Gradually his strength returned to him; the supreme, triumphant strength that filled him whenever he had fulfilled the ancient need. Hungry now with a very different passion, his lips slid upward to meet Venetia's.

She kissed his mouth. It was sticky with blood, the metallic saltiness which would normally have made her retch with horror. Here, now, it excited her beyond belief. Maddened with need, she clawed at Esteban's belt, unfastening it, unzipping his trousers, taking out what she most desperately desired.

Tearing off her robe, she offered herself to him; and he pulled her astride his soaring prick.

'My Venetia,' he breathed. 'My queen of night. My only and my ever. My eternal one . . .'

His hands slid down her body, parting the petals of her secret flower; and he slid into her with a silent ecstasy, a sublime smoothness that took him right up to the hilt. At the first thrust his cock-tip nudged against the neck of Venetia's womb, and she felt a spasm of profoundest need ripple through her.

'I am beginning to understand,' she whispered to him. And she bent to kiss him again as their sweat-soaked bodies began slowly sliding over each other, drinking in the sweetness of purest sex.

There was a sublime electricity in their coupling; an intensity which Venetia had not experienced since that night in the garden of Esteban's villa, when he had offered her the gift – and the curse – of eternity. As his beautiful, marble-smooth penis slid between her thighs, she rubbed herself long and hard against his pubic bone, willing the pleasure to last, joining him on the very edge of pleasure and praying that they might remain there for ever.

Esteban smoothed his hands down the gentle curve of her back and slipped his index finger between her buttocks, stroking and scratching the rosebud sphincter of her anus.

'Blossom for me,' he murmured, kissing her throat with infinite gentleness as they moved together, harmonising the rhythm of their passion. 'Open yourself, give me your sweetness . . .'

Rolling onto his side, Esteban possessed her with long, slow thrusts, all the time kissing and licking her breasts and throat. She felt the need building up inside her, carrying her to paradise; and at last she found the strength to trust Esteban, to open herself to him utterly, to offer him her complete vulnerability.

He kissed her mouth as they climaxed together, the sweet groan of his orgasm shuddering through her as their bodies met and their essences mingled in unique alchemy.

As dawn approached, Venetia awoke and rolled onto her back. Dark smears of dried blood on her skin reminded her of what had passed. For a second she panicked, putting her hand to her throat. But he had not harmed her. She found nothing there but the memory of Esteban's gentle kiss.

Propping herself up on one elbow, she bent over him. Kissed him. His eyes opened.

With a gasp, she drew back. Esteban's eyes were no longer black and glassy as polished jet. They were yellow as a wolf's. Pushing her gently away, he sat up, sniffing the air like a wild animal.

'Esteban . . .' She drew away. 'Esteban, what is it?'

'Danger,' he murmured. 'There is danger close by.'

And a second later, before her eyes, he vanished into thin air.

Dawn was coming up over the mountains as Gabriel and Ismail toiled along the treacherous road. To the left, the rocks and scree rose up a sheer slope too dangerous for any but an expert or a mountain goat to climb. To the right, the narrow track fell away hundreds of feet to the scrubby valley below.

Gabriel dismounted from his horse and turned to confront Ismail, who was struggling to lead a pack mule up the steep ascent. He looked hot, scared and unhappy. 'Idiot,' Gabriel snapped. 'Can you do nothing right?'

'I am sorry, master.'

'And so you should be. If we do not make better progress we will lose their trail.'

'A thousand pardons, master. The road . . . it is very steep and we are very close to the edge . . .'

Gabriel's lip curled in disdain. 'To think that any servant of mine should be afraid. Afraid of heights! You are contemptible, Ismail, do you know that?'

Lashing out, he caught Ismail a glancing blow on the side of the head, causing him to stumble and fall to his hands and knees on the stony roadway. The pack mule bucked in alarm, and almost sent half of their provisions tumbling over the edge into the valley below.

'Imbecile! Will you obey me now? Will you?'

Gabriel seized Ismail by the shoulder and dragged him to his feet. But the face which looked back at him was not the sweating, cringing face of his servant Ismail. It was the face of someone who filled him with vicious rage and just a touch of fear . . .

160

'You know, Gabriel, you really ought to be more careful,' remarked Esteban with an ironic half-smile, detaching himself with ease from Gabriel's grasp. 'It's a long way down. You might fall.'

Gabriel took a step back, momentarily thrown off balance. 'Esteban? Esteban, my enemy,' he hissed. 'Give me back what belongs to me.'

Esteban laughed. 'And what might that be, Gabriel?' he enquired. 'Your foul and festering soul, perhaps?'

He parried the blow with ease and a strength which both astonished and enraged Gabriel.

'Give me back the book.'

'The book is not what you seek, Engelhart. It is not the *Lore of Madali*. It is an old diary, of no use or value to you.'

Gabriel drew back his lips in a sneer of contempt. 'Once again you seek to trick me.'

'I have never tricked or cheated you. I only refused you that which you had no right to demand.'

Gabriel stepped forward, his face very close to Esteban's, his handsome features contorted with hatred. 'Give me back the English girl. She is not for you, she belongs to me now . . .'

Esteban shook his head. 'She is not yours to possess, Gabriel. Nor is she mine. Venetia has made her choice, and her choice is to be as far away from you as possible.' He allowed himself a half-smile. 'But then, Venetia Fellowes is a highly intelligent woman.'

Gabriel lunged forward, enraged by Esteban's calm composure, his aristocratic disdain. But Esteban was ready for him, catching him by the

161

throat with one powerful hand. And seconds later, he found himself dangling over a sheer drop, Esteban's stranglehold the only thing between him and oblivion.

He struggled for breath, but Esteban was not listening to his protests. 'Leave here, Engelhart,' he whispered. 'Leave here and never return. Or the next time, I may forget myself and kill you.'

When Gabriel came to his senses, he was lying in the dirt, the pack mule licking his face and Ismail standing over him, his ugly little face twisted with fear.

'Master, master, what ails you? You are sick?'

'Only of your incompetence,' replied Gabriel, rubbing his bruised throat. 'Which is why I am sending you back to Tunis, and continuing my journey alone.'

'Master! You cannot . . .'

But Gabriel was not listening. He was thinking of Esteban's arrogant threats, and the sweet revenge which had been so cruelly stolen from his grasp.

A'shah looked up in alarm when Venetia and Esteban returned to the camp together, Venetia with a bandage of ripped cloth wrapped round her forearm.

'Something bad has happened?'

'Nothing,' said Venetia hastily. 'I . . . fell and cut myself.'

'Let me look.'

Reluctantly, Venetia allowed A'shah to peel away the makeshift bandage. Her tone did not change, but her eyes registered surprise, perhaps suspicion.

'It looks more like a knife cut.'

'Does it? That's funny.'

A'shah looked from Venetia to Esteban and concluded that questions were pointless. 'I will dress it with special herbs. Wounds can turn bad very quickly in this climate. You should be more careful.'

Venetia looked at Esteban, wishing he would explain but knowing that he wouldn't. One moment he had spoken of 'danger', the next, he had vanished into thin air. Or had he? Had she imagined it all? Because when she had woken up a second time, still lying on the dusty grass in the gully, he had been there beside her, as though he had been there all night long.

They set off early, before dawn had turned into the full bloom of day, and before the furnace heat had begun to wilt the crispness of the mountain air.

Up here in the mountains was a different world, thought Venetia. Certainly very different from Valazur with its Riviera gamblers, millionaires and starlets; and more different still from the world of Gabriel Engelhart. When she thought of him she felt unsettled, uneasy; not quite certain that they had seen the last of him. And what if they returned to the 'real' world and he caught up with them, demanded to know why Venetia had suddenly upped and left him?

Her train of thought was broken by Esteban, laying his hand on her arm. 'See, Venetia. There, just ahead.'

A'shah was riding a few yards in front of them. Beyond her, Venetia made out the shape of something rocky, half-overgrown, but definitely man-made. A tense excitement tightened her stomach muscles.

'Is it . . .?'

Esteban shook his head. 'I don't know. But remember what the book said . . . about the gateway to a hidden valley . . .'

The gateway. Venetia recalled the spidery handwriting in the diary of Marcus Almenius: 'And when I was all but dead from thirst, I came upon a gateway, carved with the shapes of men and beasts in pleasures carnal and corporeal . . .'

They walked slowly forward. The passage of years had not been kind to the stonework, and some of the stones had crumbled or cracked and fallen. But the archway was still clearly visible, each yellow-grey stone richly carved with a freize depicting men, women and fantastical beasts, copulating in an orgy of sensual indulgence.

Flowers and soft grass grew at the base of the gateway, and through it Venetia could make out a steep, grassy slope dotted with trees.

'Will you come with us?'

'I can go no further,' replied A'shah. There was the ghost of fear in her face. 'This place . . . no, I cannot.'

Esteban and Venetia watched her mount her horse and ride away, glancing back only once before disappearing round a bend in the mountain road. Esteban searched Venetia's face for a sign of doubt. 'You are certain?'

'You know I am.'

'We can still turn back.'

'Things can never go back, Esteban. Only forward.'

And stepping through the gateway, they walked together down the grassy slope. Into the unknown.

Chapter Ten

VENETIA EXAMINED THE inscription on the gateway. It was barely discernible now after the ravages of time and weather. Esteban watched her picking out the letters painstakingly, slowly speaking the words as she translated them.

'It's in very old, very corrupt type of Latin. It says, "Alexander did not come this way, nor Gilgamesh." ' She turned to Esteban. 'But what does it mean?'

Esteban shook his head. 'That, *ma petite anglaise*, I do not know. Perhaps we shall discover its meaning.'

They walked on together. The gateway had been situated in a narrow gap between two steep slopes. Once on the other side of it, they saw that the grassy earth sloped sharply away, forming a path which led round the side of the mountain. Dusty grass, stunted trees, a few pale flowers were all the vegetation here. There seemed nothing remarkable, nothing to show that this place had ever been anything but a wasteland; a staging post on the road to nowhere.

Then they turned a corner.

'Esteban, look! Just look . . .'

Esteban could hardly do anything else. He stood stock-still, gazing at the vista suddenly spread out before them.

They were standing at the head of a valley, deep and green and almost tropical in its lushness. It was the abundance of water that struck you first – the sheer moistness of this place, so incongruously placed in the heart of a rocky desert.

Gazing down through trees that swayed in a soft, warm wind, Venetia made out a broad, lazy river in the valley bottom, winding its way sinuously between green-clad banks whose leafy glades rustled with unseen life.

A shower of many-coloured brightness made her look up, and she saw a cloud of huge, iridescent butterflies, dancing above her head, wheeling and tumbling in the moist, warm air.

'This place,' murmured Esteban. 'I have seen it before . . . somewhere . . . somehow.'

Venetia looked at him sharply. 'You have been here before? But surely . . .'

He put up his hand. 'No. No, I have never been here. At least . . .' He passed a hand across his forehead. 'I believe that I have dreamed it.'

'Let's find out more about this place.'

Filled with a breathless excitement, Venetia took the initiative and stepped forward. Birds sang in leafy treetops, their clear song stirring the sleepy air. Flowers carpeted the grass at their feet. It was all unbelievably lush. A dream. Something not quite real.

Bright lianas hung across a bend in the

pathway. Venetia reached out and touched the curtain of hanging foliage, a bright-green creeper swinging lazily down the side of a rocky face. Behind it, she glimpsed craggy rocks, running with water. Hot and dusty, Venetia plunged in her hands. The water was cold and so clear, so sweet. Beyond, she found herself looking into a darkness suffused with sparks of light, and heard a soft, distant roar of thunder.

'It's a waterfall!' she exclaimed with delight, and she stepped through the leafy curtain into the wet green twilight beyond.

'Venetia, be careful . . .'

'It's all right, Esteban, it's quite safe. It's . . . it's so beautiful, I can hardly believe it.'

She stretched out her hand and, filled with misgivings, Esteban joined her. Before them a waterfall crashed down from some unseen height, the water fracturing into a million crystal drops as it thundered into the deep pool.

As they stood before the waterfall, letting the spray moisten their faces, making their clothes cling to their bodies, a red and gold parakeet scythed through the twilight, crying and shrilling as it cut through the water and emerged on the other side, a stem of coral-pink blossom on its beak.

'Look, Esteban . . . look.' She caught the blossom as it fell from the bird's beak. 'It's almost as if . . .'

'I know, Venetia. Almost as if this place is welcoming us.' So why do I feel uneasy? thought Esteban.

'There are animals here too – look, do you see?'

Esteban turned slowly. No. It couldn't be, it made no sense. Sitting on its haunches beside the waterfall was an ocelot, its spotted coat dappled like leaves spotted with sunlight and shadow. An ocelot? Here, on the Syrian border? Parakeets? Butterflies as big as saucers? It was like stepping into the middle of some over-the-top dream. And yet. And yet, this was the most beautiful, the most erotic place he had ever been. He ached with the need to take Venetia in his arms and make passionate love to her.

He took Venetia's hand. 'Bathe with me.'

'Here?'

'Here, in the waterfall.' He pressed his lips against Venetia, his hot, hungry body communicating its need to her. 'You are my hunger and my thirst, Venetia. Only you can staunch the burning heat within me.'

Gently, he unwrapped the bandage from Venetia's arm, and peeled away the herbs A'shah had used as a poultice. The flesh was clean but only half-healed, still tender, and Venetia winced as he touched it.

'Be still, *ma petite*.' Esteban bent to place a kiss upon Venetia's forearm, his lips touching the wounded flesh lightly, for the briefest second. But in that second, Venetia felt a rush of icy coldness running from shoulders to fingertip, a dart of electricity, carrying away the badness and the corruption.

He straightened up. 'You are healed now.'

Venetia looked down at her arm. Before her eyes the cut was healing to a scar, and the purple of the scar fading to red, then dusky pink and white. It was disappearing even as she looked at it!

Astonished, she turned to Esteban. The look in

his eyes was soft and distant, as though clouded with some unshared pain. 'How . . .?'

'I have taken your hurt upon myself.' He silenced her protests with a kiss. 'No, no, it is nothing to me, such a small thing. Now, will you bathe with me, *ma chère*?' He laughed. 'Or must I make you do my bidding?'

She laughed with him. He was not often so light-hearted, so teasingly attractive. The darkness seemed to melt away from him, his eyes sparkling with mirth as he tore off his shirt and kicked off his black leather boots.

'Oh, I don't know. I think you should make me . . .'

Esteban stood before her, clad only in the tight black trousers which accentuated the thick, curving line of his swelling penis. Venetia felt her nipples tingle and stiffen, her sex swelling and plumping with the delicious anticipation of what must come.

He was irresistible to her, this dark, mysterious lover who was often distant, at times arrogantly self-possessed, yet so tenderly passionate. He was her lifeblood, her need, her addiction. As he gathered her up in his arms, she felt her heart soar with the adrenaline rush of delicious danger. He whispered in her ear as he bit and licked her earlobe.

'You intoxicate my senses, *petite anglaise*. What you do to me is beyond endurance . . .'

The next thing she knew, he had swept her off her feet in his strong arms. Still fully clothed, she wriggled and shrieked with mad, drunken laughter. 'Esteban, Esteban, *put me down*!'

He laughed; a warm, husky laugh which sent

shivers of need rushing through her belly, her limbs, her willing sex.

'No,' he replied quite simply, hoisting her up so that he could plant a kiss on her lips. 'No, I don't think I shall.'

'Put me down, put me down!'

'You're sure that's what you want, *petite anglaise*?'

'Yes, yes!'

'Very well . . .'

And all of a sudden he jumped, still carrying Venetia in his arms, into the deep pool at the base of the waterfall.

Down, down, down they sank together, their bodies closely entwined, their mouths locked in a kiss that seemed as if it would never end. A wonderful, breathless, passionate, eternal kiss.

Venetia felt no need to fight for air, no need to do anything but kiss and caress her lover. In those fleeting moments, Esteban became her life, her breath, her whole existence; her past and her tomorrow. And then, just as suddenly, the greens and cold blues and cool amber of the water mingled and brightened, and they shot towards the surface, exploding into light with laughter and kisses.

'Beast!' she squealed.

'*Chère bête . . . chère petite sauvage . . .*'

She clawed at his back as they tumbled together in the cool green water, her wet clothes diaphanous, clinging to the contours of her body. Her nipples were hard as stones, her pubis a swollen mound beneath the clinging gauzy fabric. Cool wetness soaked through her skirt and into the warm haven of her sex, meeting the hot ooze of her need, caressing her swollen clitoris with secret, lascivious fingers.

They kissed, the crystal-clear water flooding their mouths as their lips met. They drank, and the elixir filled them with an exhilarating warmth.

Venetia looked into Esteban's eyes. His dark lashes were wet with tiny, bright droplets. She wanted to kiss them away.

'I want you, *petite anglaise*,' he murmured. 'I must have you.'

His hands began tearing at Venetia's clothes. She panted with need, her body writhing as his strong fingers pulled away her shirt, baring her heavy, golden breasts. The water buoyed them up, carrying them to the surface of the water like pink-tipped lilies, offering them to the sunlight to kiss them and make them bloom.

Greenish shadows fluttered and danced across Esteban's bare torso, making him seem like some fantastical beast born out of the raw power of nature. Venetia could feel his heart pounding as he pulled her close and began massaging the firm globes of her buttocks, so closely moulded by the wet, twisted fabric of her skirt.

Their bodies locked in an embrace, they tumbled over and over in the water, splashing and laughing, blissful with a childish, carefree lust. As Esteban unfastened the button holding up her skirt, Venetia suddenly pulled away.

'If you want me, catch me . . .'

Her eyes danced with the secret light of lust. She was teasing, tantalising, revelling in the tranquil, sensual power of this place.

Esteban watched her strike out across the lake at the base of the waterfall, her skirt floating away like a pink shadow as her naked skin flashed pale gold beneath the luminous water. Throwing back his head, he laughed. Water droplets shook from his wet hair like a sparkling halo. He could not remember a time when he had felt so good. So . . . so free. Here, for at least a few, precious moments, it was as if the curse upon him had no meaning.

He followed her, his powerful body scything through the water, his arms reaching out to grab her.

She turned, laughing, her lips wet and glossy. He seized hold of her and the waters engulfed them, caressing; a soundless cocoon of greens and blues and many-coloured brightness where only their passion existed.

When they broke the surface again, they were underneath the waterfall, its power thundering about them, the water hitting the surface of the pool so hard that it sprang up again in a fine mist. Esteban took Venetia's hand and guided her through the deafening curtain of water, his strength pulling them through.

Venetia could hardly breathe, could not move against the force of the cascade. But Esteban's fingers were holding hers tightly, drawing her on, making her trust and believe and abandon herself to his will.

At last they burst through the curtain of water into the silence beyond. Venetia blinked and shook the wetness from her eyes, gasping for breath. Here, there was no sound at all save for the distant rumble of the waterfall. They were between the tumbling cascade and the sheer rock face. Tiny, scarlet-coloured birds were sipping nectar from pink and yellow flowers growing on the rocks; dragonflies with huge, shimmering, diaphanous wings skimming just above the surface of the water. The air was flower-scented, cool and clear; each indrawn breath a tiny orgasm of innocent pleasure.

A sandy bank sloped gently beneath the surface of the pool. Esteban swam towards it, leading Venetia there. Her heart pounded in her chest. She wanted him, ached for him, longed to worship his body with hands and mouth and sex.

Together they tumbled, panting, onto the wet sand. Cool water lapped at their legs as they lay there, but they paid it no heed. Esteban pulled Venetia on top of him and gently pushed the tendrils of wet hair out of her eyes.

'Here, there is no darkness,' he whispered. 'Can you feel it? All that exists is pleasure.'

He pulled her mouth down to his and kissed her. She tasted of nectar, intoxicating and sweet. And in a sudden ache of need, he rolled her onto her back.

'Take me,' she pleaded, her tongue flicking across her lips, her eyes full of need. Her fingers reached out, stroking and caressing the long, hard bulge of Esteban's penis, so tightly kissed by the wet fabric of his trousers.

Esteban's eyes closed in ecstasy at the sureness, the lightness of her touch. Only she knew the secret ways to transport him into the divine madness of inexorable desire. Gently, firmly, regretfully, he brushed her fingers away, carrying them to his lips and kissing them.

'First, I must pay my own homage, *chère sauvage*.'

Sliding down her body, he marked his progress with a long line of kisses, each one lingering and moist, a butterfly's wing brushing the skin, sipping its nectar then moving on.

At last he reached her navel. He thrust the tip of his tongue inside, slowly and languidly, like a lazy insect seeking out nectar. Venetia cried out and clutched at him, twisting handfuls of his blue-black hair about her tormented fingers. 'No . . . no, I can't bear it.'

'Patience, *ma petite. Sois tranquille* . . .'

He began licking and probing again. Venetia shivered and arched her back. The sensation was unbearable, incredibly intimate. It felt as though Esteban had searched out the very epicentre of her sex and was running it through with the finest, the most exquisite silver needles. His tongue twisted, probed, withdrew and then came back again, exploring new and undreamed-of worlds of intense sensation.

When he withdrew for the last time, Venetia was moaning helplessly, winding and twisting and gently tilting her hips.

'Oh Esteban. Esteban, no more, I can't . . .'

But Esteban was kissing the line of fine, golden hairs which led down from Venetia's navel to the luxuriant mound of her pubic hair. He breathed in her scent, his senses drunk on the fragrance of her wetness, the irresistible mixture of purest springwater and honeydew.

'You grow more beautiful by the hour, *petite anglaise*. You smell of sex. You have ensnared me with the wondrous scent of your sex . . .'

His words, low and soft, punctuated his kisses on her belly. She felt him working down, with unbearable slowness, until his lips met the wet curls cresting the swell of her pubic bone. His first kiss on her mount of Venus had the brutal intensity of an electric shock, and her backside lifted as every muscle in her body tensed, spasmed, collapsed back onto the soft, wet sand.

Esteban felt it too. He felt every shiver of ecstasy, every agonised spasm of pleasure that rippled through Venetia's body. For that was his blessing and his curse; to feel as she felt, to know her pain, to share her ecstasy.

He bent over her, softly stroking her thighs apart. 'Open for me, *ma petite*. Blossom for me.'

Her thighs relaxed and her legs parted, revealing the sex-swollen pout of her pussy-lips. He ran the tip of his index finger along the dusky pink line and she opened to him like a ripe fruit, bursting with sweet juice and soft pink flesh.

The hunger was at the back of his mind; a dark shadow looking over his shoulder; the sight of Venetia's womanhood bringing back the ache of need. It would be so simple, so blissful, to kiss her and drink her and empty her of life. To take what he longed to have, to make her his. To bring her out of the light and into the darkness – his darkness. The all-encircling darkness of the vampire.

He steadied his breathing, cursing the vile whispering in his head. *Take her, take her, she is yours now. She can be yours for ever . . .*

No. He would never yield to the darkness, not even if it cost him Venetia, the only woman he had ever truly cared for. Summoning the light to fill him, he bent to worship at her secret spring, and drank down the sweetness of her innocence.

In the haze of pleasure, Venetia abandoned herself to Esteban, banishing the fear, welcoming the kiss of his lips and tongue on the flower-stalk of her sex.

'Yes. Yes, oh yes, Esteban. Don't stop, please don't ever stop . . .'

At the point of orgasm he entered her, his penis like a rod of white-hot steel, his body feverish and hungry; their embrace so close that they were no longer two beings but one. And as their climax shuddered through them, Esteban wondered how much longer he could sustain the strength to resist his deepest, darkest passion.

That night, they pitched camp on the valley floor, in the shade of towering trees that whispered as the night wind caressed their branches.

They huddled together around the bonfire they had built from dried leaves and twigs. They had no need of the warmth it produced, but everywhere they could hear the sound of animals calling to each other.

'Do you see them?' Venetia snuggled into the crook of Esteban's arm. He held her close, his eyes scanning the darkness beyond the circle of yellow light. 'They're watching us, just waiting . . .'

'Nothing will harm you. Nothing.'

In the darkness, countless bright eyes watched and waited; a spreading circle of unwinking light, luminous in the flickering firelight.

Something moved in the darkness; a scurrying, scrabbling noise which made Venetia gasp and seize Esteban's arm. 'Something . . . did you hear it?'

'It is nothing.' Esteban concealed his own concern from his lover. He too had seen the dark shapes concealed in the dappled branches of the trees, heard the cries cutting through the air. Who could tell what might be here, waiting to prey upon them?

A small shape scurried forward.

'Esteban!'

It was a bat-eared fox, its muzzle pink and wet, its eyes large as a bush-baby's. It scurried into the encampment, darting forward on spider-thin legs to steal a piece of fruit; and then, just as quickly, it was gone.

Angry now, Esteban got to his feet. His eyes seemed to glint like polished steel in the firelight. He raised his hand to the night sky in a clenched fist.

'Begone. Creatures of the night, I command you, begone.'

At the sound of Esteban's voice the eyes blinked, darkened, then disappeared as the animals slunk away. A low howling shimmered through the still night air, then there was silence. An eerie, uneasy, unpleasant silence which Venetia longed to be broken.

Esteban turned back to Venetia. 'The beasts will obey me. They will not harm you, I swear it.'

But not all the eyes had disappeared. To Venetia, it seemed as if some were actually getting closer.

And she could have sworn they looked human.

Three days passed, and Venetia and Esteban explored the rest of the valley. They found a few small buildings, long ruined and deserted, many

177

unknown species of flowers, fruit and insects. But no one who could help them in their quest.

'Nothing,' sighed Venetia, sinking down onto a rock.

Esteban sat down beside her, pushing back his mass of dark hair. 'We will find what we seek.'

'But Esteban, we've followed everything in the diary. Everything. To the letter. Do you think Marcus Almenius made the whole thing up?'

'We found the gateway. And this valley.'

'But nothing else. No settlement, no people, nothing. Perhaps we should turn back.'

'I at least must not give up.' Esteban's stone-black eyes rested on the middle distance, as though he could almost catch sight of something beyond mortal perception. 'I cannot, too much rests upon it. But you, Venetia . . .' He let out a long, slow current of breath. 'I cannot and will not hold you to this quest.'

She knelt beside him, her fingers stroking his thigh through his trousers. 'Where you go, I go.'

'Even if I lead you into danger?'

'I've never shunned danger, you know that.'

Esteban began massaging Venetia's shoulders, rubbing away the tension in her back and neck, caressing her as he spoke his thoughts. 'I do not understand it. The diary spoke of a settlement . . . and yet there is nothing here.'

'Could there have been a village which isn't here any more? Those ruins . . .'

'Venetia, you are the archaeologist. You have read the diary and you have seen what I have seen. There is nothing here that resembles what Almenius described, no sign that many people have ever lived here.' His hands worked gently at

Venetia's shoulders. 'But we will find the town . . . we must.'

Venetia turned to look at him over her shoulder. 'We will.' Her lips curved into a smile. 'What's the hurry anyway? Its beautiful here. It makes me . . . horny.'

Her fingers stroked up the inner surface of Esteban's thigh, reaching the hypersensitive crease between thigh and balls. He groaned with pleasure as her fingers brushed the flesh, and his hand covered hers.

'Not here . . .'

She looked up, surprised. 'Why?'

'I don't know . . . there's something . . . I can *feel* something.' He breathed in the scented air. Nothing but the perfumes of flowers and animal scents, musky and sweet. Perhaps he was imagining it. He took his hand away, and allowed Venetia to unzip his flies, taking out the glossy, ripening fruit of his cock.

'I want you, I'm so thirsty for you,' she breathed, and parting her lips she put out her tongue and began to lick.

The sound was a tiny one; scarcely more than a rustle of leaves in the undergrowth. An animal, scurrying through the leaves. Then Esteban heard it again, and this time Venetia heard it too. The sound of something . . . no, *someone*, crying out as though startled.

Venetia and Esteban turned and looked in the direction of the noise.

'Someone . . . did you see?'

Esteban nodded. With his acute vision, he had seen more than she. He had glimpsed the dark, lithe shape of a human figure, running away through the undergrowth.

'Should we . . .?'

Esteban leapt to his feet, zipping his flies. 'We must follow. We have no choice.'

And they began running, scrambling, chasing through the trees and bushes, Venetia panting and gasping as she struggled to keep up with Esteban's long strides.

The shape disappeared then reappeared, a fast-moving shadow among many shadows, almost lost in the shifting patterns of sunlight among the close-packed leaves.

'There.' Esteban pointed to a gap between the trees. Venetia followed, pushing through the foliage to discover not the wooded glade she had expected, but the entrance to a cave.

'It's very dark . . .'

'Follow me.'

'I can't see . . .'

'Hold my hand. The dark holds no fears for me.'

As they stepped inside, Venetia became aware that the darkness was not quite complete. Somewhere in the far distance a muted orange light glowed, scarcely more than a soft haze in the blackness.

Venetia stumbled on loose rocks, grateful for Esteban's firm grip. She knew that she must trust him to find a safe path through the darkness.

The cave narrowed, and Esteban had to stoop, helping Venetia along, his strong hands holding her when she slipped, her fingers scrabbling helplessly on the wet rocks.

'It's too narrow, Esteban, I can't go any further.'

He held her close against him, stilling the frantic pounding of her heart with gentle kisses.

'A little further, *petite anglaise*. A little further, then no more. Trust me . . .'

Further, further, further. The orange smear of light became a haze, then a blur, and finally a glow.

'There's something . . . an opening,' gasped Venetia.

'Yes.' Esteban stopped in his tracks, his grip about her waist tightening.

'What's the matter? What can you see?'

He swore softly under his breath, Spanish curses of astonishment that came tumbling out. '*Madre de dios* . . .'

He walked slowly forward, into the light, Venetia a step behind, her hand tightly clasped in his. She gasped as she emerged from the cave and her eyes became accustomed to the soft, many-coloured glow.

'No! It can't be . . .'

At first, she could not believe it. Her eyes must be deceiving her. This was some dream, some phantasmagoria invented by a disordered mind. But beautiful, so beautiful . . .

It was a town. No, an incredible city, but from the rock walls of a gigantic chasm, driven through the heart of the mountain. It towered above and below their feet, rising hundreds of feet towards the distant sky, where huge outcrops of many-coloured quartz caught the sun and reflected it down into the city, filling it with a rainbow of light.

And there were people. People watching them from corners, eyes wide, watchful. Advancing towards them, reaching out to touch the two strangers who had stepped into the middle of this otherworldly world.

181

Chapter Eleven

A LOW WHISPER ran round the strange, rock-hewn city, echoing as it was reflected off the quartz-studded walls.

At first, Venetia could not see the people, though she knew they must be there, watching. Then slowly, tentatively, they began to emerge into the light, their eyes wide with curiosity.

They were a tall, handsome race; rather dark with pale olive skins that shimmered in the waterfall of many-coloured light. The men wore short tunics kilted with leather belts, and turquoise-coloured jewellery on their arms and at their throats. The woman were slightly-built, their hair cropped short in a boyish style. They dressed in filmy sarongs which left much of their bodies bare, revealing gaudy painted designs swirled over their smooth skin.

'This place . . .' gasped Venetia. 'It's so much bigger than the settlement in Marcus Almenius's diary . . .'

'Many hundreds of years have passed.' Esteban surveyed the scene, shading his eyes against the shimmer of light. Eyes watched, looked back at him, spellbound, curious yet not hostile. He turned back to Venetia. 'We must not hope for too much. These people may have forgotten what they knew, if it is true that they ever knew anything at all. And once they know who and what I am, they may not be well disposed towards us.'

'I don't see what choice we have. We have to take that chance – we can't go back now.'

Esteban pursed his lips, resisting a smile. 'Your courage is equalled only by your recklessness,' he commented.

Esteban led Venetia forward, into the full glare of day. They walked slowly down a flight of steps cut into the rock, until they emerged on to a rose-pink terrace. From there, they had a clearer view over the town; and Venetia saw that it consisted of a dizzying mass of tunnels, staircases and gateways, cut into the rock. There was no way of knowing how far it extended, or what lay beyond the enigmatic, rocky façades.

Together they descended into the heart of the town. Slowly, figures came forward to greet them. Venetia tried to read their expressions, silently praying that they would be friendly. She let out a startled cry as a girl reached out to touch her hair. The girl made a strange, low purring sound like a curious animal as her long, tattooed hands smoothed over the wavy blonde mane.

Another girl, very young and pretty, reached out tentative fingers to touch Esteban, but he rounded on her, pushing her away.

'Esteban,' warned Venetia. 'Esteban, be careful . . . we mustn't offend them.'

'I will not – I cannot – tolerate their touch on my flesh. It causes me pain, it awakens the blood hunger . . .'

By now, a circle of onlookers had gathered, and Venetia decided that she must do her best to communicate with them. She placed a hand on her breast. 'Venetia. Venetia, yes?'

The eyes narrowed slightly, the heads tilting forward, listening.

'Venetia,' repeated the pretty girl who had touched Esteban. 'Ven-ee-sha.'

'Esteban.' Venetia touched Esteban's arm. 'Esteban.'

The girl's lips curved into a smile of pure lust, and she reached out to him, offering a flower from her hair.

'Esteban . . . Esteban . . .' Her voice was a silky sigh, and Venetia experienced a sudden pang of mad, possessive jealousy. She could almost have laughed at the ridiculousness of it, if it had not felt so strong, so bitter, so real. She watched as the girl pointed to herself. 'Pernette.'

Esteban took the flower from the girl's hand. For a few seconds it seemed to sparkle in his hand, as though it were made of frosted glass. But as he stroked his fingers along the stem, it dissolved into a cloud of shimmering dust which drifted to the ground about his feet. The crowd drew back with an 'ahhh' of astonishment, entranced yet uneasy.

Venetia was so preoccupied with trying to coax back the girl that she did not notice the two men approaching.

Esteban was aware of their presence long before Venetia. He raised his head, his eyes filled

184

with a strange and troubled brightness. 'They have come for us.'

Venetia looked up to see two men pushing their way through the crowd. They were different in appearance from the other townsfolk, their bodies muscular and brown, their expressions blank and unwelcoming. They were wearing armour made from small plates of a dull, black metal, and conical helmets which reminded Venetia of Byzantine armour she had once catalogued at the British Museum. At their belts, double-edged sword-blades glittered.

Heart pounding, Venetia shrank away.

Esteban drew her to his side. 'We must go with them.'

'No, Esteban. Esteban, I'm afraid . . .'

He kissed her on her forehead and spoke softly to her.

'Welcome the fear and use it, Venetia. Fear is a power like any other.'

'I can't!'

'You can, Venetia. There is so much that you can do. Within you there is a strength you do not yet recognise or understand. Live with the fear, confront it as I have confronted it through seven long centuries.'

And together, they followed the two men out of the square, towards a small, square gateway in the rock face.

They passed through the gateway and into the first of many rooms. Despite her apprehension, Venetia found herself excited by what she saw. Each room was hewn from solid rock, yet the workmanship was exquisite, the decoration not quite like anything she had ever seen before. It was European and yet not European, exotic but sometimes oddly familiar.

Crossing a third room, the walls narrowed to form a passageway; then suddenly widened again, opening into an immense hall with bright frescoes of dancing girls and animals painted on its smooth sandstone walls. Venetia looked up, and saw that there were deep shafts cut high up in the walls, flooding the hall with sunlight.

There were three people in the hall, two handsome women of perhaps thirty-five, and an older man in purple robes, with a circlet of twisted gold on his curly, oiled hair. They were sitting together on gilded chairs, raised up on a dais. Town elders perhaps, thought Venetia. The man spoke in a deep, sonorous voice.

'*Soyez les bienvenus.*'

Venetia stared, open-mouthed. French? He was speaking to them in French! Heavily-accented and archaic French, it was true, but there was no mistaking its origin.

Esteban seemed unsurprised. He inclined his head in a deferential nod.

'*Vous nous honorez, messire.*'

The Elder nodded to the two guards and clapped his hands. 'You may retire,' he said in his archaic French. Then he turned his attentions to Venetia. 'You are very striking,' he commented dispassionately.

'I . . . thank you.'

'You and your companion must also be very resourceful. Few have succeeded in finding this place since our forefathers came here, many centuries ago.'

He contemplated Venetia in silence for a few

moments, as though lost in thought. It was Venetia who broke the silence. 'Sir . . . What is this place? Who are these people?'

'I am Baudouin, Vizier of the ancient city of Tamezion.' He paused. 'My ancestors were French soldiers, pursued into these mountains by Saracen warriors. They remained and settled here, intermarrying with the natives of this place and sharing their great wisdom.' Baudouin looked from Venetia to Esteban and back again. 'Now you must tell me why you have come here.'

Esteban stepped forward. '*Messire Baudouin* . . . I am Esteban and this is my companion, Venetia. We have come to plead for your help.'

The Vizier turned his quiet brown eyes on Esteban. His expression did not change. 'I see. And why should my people wish to help you?'

Esteban felt impatience rising in his throat. 'You have helped others. Why not us?'

A flicker of interest passed across Baudouin's face, as though he had glimpsed the darkness beyond Esteban's impassive eyes. 'Tell me, *Monsieur* Esteban. And answer me truly. Are you touched by the blood curse?'

'These seven hundred years and more I have lived in torment, unable to die, unable to live as a mortal man.' His eyes glittered. 'You must help us. You cannot refuse us.'

Baudouin exchanged glances with the two women at his side. 'We do not have to do anything. On the contrary, *Monsieur* Esteban, it is for you to provide us with explanations.' He looked from Esteban to Venetia and back again. 'You and she are lovers?'

Esteban cast down his eyes, unable to meet the

Vizier's gaze. 'To my eternal shame and my honour's damnation.'

Baudouin continued speaking. 'You know the danger to her? If the hunger comes upon you and you cannot control it?'

Esteban turned to Venetia, his eyes filled with shame. 'I acknowledge the weakness of my flesh and spirit. My actions do me no honour.'

Venetia cut in. 'If there is any weakness of spirit, it is mine. Esteban told me we must never meet again . . . but then we found the book, and it changed everything.'

One of the female Elders leaned forward in her chair. 'Tell me of this book.'

'It is the diary of a man called Marcus Almenius, an explorer. It tells how he came here, many years ago, and saw . . .'

Her mouth dried, the words catching in her throat. Esteban took up the story.

'It told how he saw the curing of a vampire, the casting out of the blood curse.' His coal-black eyes blazed with a new intensity, the desperation of a man who has seen into the depths of the abyss.

'That was long ago,' said the second female elder. 'Many hundreds of years, when our ancestors had not long been in Tamezion, learning the ancient wisdom.'

Venetia's brain whirled. 'Will you . . . can you help us? Do you still possess the knowledge and the skill?'

The woman shook her head slowly. 'It has been many centuries . . . in the time before we began to forget the old ways . . .'

The last vestiges of colour were draining from Esteban's face. He looked waxen, ghostlike beneath the olive veneer of his skin.

'If you cannot help us,' he said flatly, 'provide us with one night's rest and we will go from this place and never return.'

The female Elder got to her feet. 'I do not say that we cannot help you,' she said. 'Only that we cannot be sure. Have patience and stay with us a while, become our guests, let us find out what can be done for you. You will be free to move about the city as you wish.' Her eyes lighted on Esteban. They seemed to see into his very soul. 'The only law here,' she added softly, 'is that you must do no harm.'

Gabriel Engelhart followed the girl along the dark tunnel. Even in the half-light from the lantern he could see that Pernette was more than attractive. Her sinuous body twisted and turned in the shadows, her snake-hips bare but for the thin, filmy sarong she wore loosely tied about her to cover her taut belly and her small, apple-hard breasts.

The darkness began to lighten, and she swung round to face him, her face almost elfin, her eyes bright with laughter. She was flirting with him. He could read her desire in those cherry-black eyes. And that suited his purposes very well. He could use an ally and a plaything in this weird, unearthly place.

'*Nous sommes presqu'arrivés,*' she told him in her light, sing-song voice. 'We shall soon be there.'

It sounded peculiar, listening to this profoundly exotic young creature speaking to him in old-fashioned French. Not that it posed many problems for Gabriel. He spoke a couple of dozen languages, all of them fluently. And by his own reckoning, he could seduce a beautiful woman in any language.

'Lead on. Show me.'

He followed close behind her, glad that he had sent Ismail away. Ismail had his uses, but here he would only get in the way, be indiscreet, ruin everything and probably get them both killed.

'Do you know where they have taken them – the two strangers?' he asked her as they paused to rest. She purred softly as he stroked her short, thick hair.

'No, *m'sieur*. But they are somewhere in the city. I saw them before the guards took them away. The woman, she is pretty. The man, he is very beautiful . . .' She closed her eyes in pleasurable reminiscence, and Gabariel felt a stab of annoyance.

'Esteban,' he spat contemptuously. 'He is worthless slime, he is nothing. Nothing, do you hear?'

The girl's eyes widened with alarm, the eyes of a startled fawn. Realising he had overstepped the mark, Gabriel drew her to him and stifled her faint protests with a passionate kiss.

At first Pernette resisted him, her strong, lithe limbs pushing against him, her whole body rigid with fear or outrage or both. But Gabriel Engelhart was a skilful lover. He knew she would not long resist him. His mouth possessed hers, his tongue forcing its way between her lips and into the warm haven beyond. He thrilled to the taste of her, sweet and fresh, like her innocence. A transient taste, he told himself with satisfaction. Innocence could not long endure in the arms of

Gabriel Engelhart. He liked to destroy it before it had a chance to grow stale.

In the half-light their eyes met, and he knew Pernette was his for the taking. The mesmeric power of his blue eyes held her fast, making her yield to him. And all the time he was whispering to her of how it would be, of the pleasure she would feel as he entered her and took her for his own.

'M'sieur, je vous en prie . . . m'sieur, j'ai gran' peur . . .'

'Do not be afraid. What is there to be afraid of?' His voice, syrupy and smooth, soothed her fears like a cool hand smoothing across a fevered brow.

'I do not know, m'sieur. I do not know if this is right. Perhaps I should go, tell the Elders of the city . . .'

'Hush, hush. Be still.' The hypnotic modulations of his voice lulled her, stilled her breathing, relaxed the muscles in the hands that clutched at him, so greedy and yet so afraid.

The apprehension seemed to drain out of her face and her features relaxed. She almost smiled, her lips parting and the tip of her tongue flicking across them, leaving a slick of moisture that glistened in the lantern light.

'What is it that you desire of me, m'sieur?'

'I desire you, Pernette. I desire everything about you, my secret flower.'

His flingers slid down her back. Her sarong was moist with cooling sweat, clingy and so very fragile.

'I want you naked, my little flower. Naked as nature intended.'

Or the Devil, he thought to himself with a

frisson of malicious satisfaction.

'*Non! Non, j'crois pas . . .*'

She felt a return of the fear, but it was too late to change her mind. In any case, she was caught fast in the web of Gabriel's sensual intrigue. She feared him but desired him, longed for him to take her and use and devour her every bit as much as she longed for him to let her go.

Pernette's breasts rose and fell with the quickening rhythm of her breathing. Gabriel's face came closer to hers and he kissed her again, taking her breath away. Her legs felt weak, her thighs trembling and moist with the juices trickling from between her petals of her secret flower.

She felt his hands undressing her, unpinning and unwinding the loose wrap until the gauzy fabric fell away with the softest whisper and she felt the cool dampness of the air on her skin.

Together they sank to the stony bed of the cave. It was damp with trickles of brackish water, but she noticed nothing save the heat from their two bodies, mingling, kindling, flaring up into the white-hot heat of unstoppable lust.

'Such beautiful breasts,' murmured Gabriel, his thigh sliding between hers, the hardness of muscle meeting the soft springiness of her pubic mound. He took one breast in each hand, squeezing, palpating, flicking his thumbnails so that they scratched across the erect nipples.

She squealed with pleasure, writhing and bucking on the stony floor. Instinctively she thrust upwards with her pelvis, her fleshy outer labia parting as her pubic bone met Gabriel's thigh and grinding hard against it, smearing his skin with her special wetness.

He lay half-on, half-off her, his thigh between hers, his belly pressing down on hers so that the fleshy spear of his cock was trapped deliciously in a sticky prison of sweating flesh.

She was in an ecstasy of lust now, her fear forgotten, her only thought the pleasure he was giving her as he rubbed long and slow on her clitoris.

'*Je n'en puis plus, je n'en puis plus,*' she moaned as he took her to a plateau of excitement and held her there, refusing her the sweet mercy of orgasm.

'You will bear it, my love, and you will worship the cock that brings you to ecstasy.'

His voice was a caress in itself; a long, slow, sweet caress that swept over her body and made it tremble with anticipation.

'You will serve me well, my pretty one,' he smiled to himself. 'The gift of pleasure binds you to me more securely than any rope or chain. And with you to assist me, I shall soon have my revenge on Esteban and his English bitch for good and all.'

The following morning, Venetia and Esteban were summoned before the Elders once again. Guards led them down rose and amber-tinted passageways, up and down flights of steps cut into blocks of solid rose-quartz. It was all so unreal, like something out of a child's storybook. Unreal, and yet so deadly serious. For Esteban had come here to bargain for his life.

They emerged into a chamber with a high, domed ceiling made from intricately-patterned stained glass. Flickering patterns of coloured light flooded the room, dancing on the many smooth stone pillars and the mosaic floor, depicting a girl dressed in white, pursued through a forest by many-headed, fantastical beasts.

The younger of the two female Elders, Aduca, summoned them into the chamber. It was empty, save for a low dais, on which stood a simple lectern of carved wood.

'Greetings.' Aduca walked before them to the lectern, followed by a young girl Venetia recognised as Pernette, the one who had touched Esteban when they first arrived in the city. 'I have brought you here to show you something. Our Book of Ancient Wisdom. In your world, those who have looked upon it call it the *Lore of Madali . . .*'

Venetia gasped. The *Lore of Madali* – here, in this lost city?

'But . . .' she murmured.

Aduca lifted her hand to impose silence. 'This book contains all the wisdom of Tamezion,' she explained, 'gathered together in pictures and symbols, coded so that only the elect may understand our secrets. It also contains the last recorded account of a successful lifting of the blood curse.' She turned to the girl by her side. 'You may open the book, Pernette.'

'*Oui, madame.*'

The girl crossed to the lectern and opened the book, marking the page with a length of purple ribbon. Venetia stared down at it. It looked so . . . insignificant, just a collection of yellowed parchments, roughly sewn together. But just as in the photograph she had seen, the pages were filled with exquisite pictures, erotic symbols, tiny writing . . .

'You both read old Latin?'

Venetia nodded.

'Good. You will see that the relevant page has been translated.'

Her head spinning, Venetia stepped forward. Esteban did not move. Now that the moment of truth had arrived he felt paralysed, impotent. His life, his death, his torment . . . all might depend upon the turn of a dusty page.

Venetia bowed her head and read from the book. 'And the elders of the city did bring forth a holy man afflicted of the blood curse, which man was much pained by the hunger. And they bound him, for they were fearful of his strength and the darkness in his eyes . . .'

The darkness in his eyes. Venetia shivered with recognition. How many times had she seen that look in Esteban's eyes? The dark shadow, the pain, the hunger? The danger that waited patiently for her behind the innocent cloak of a kiss.

She read on, her blood chilling as she followed the course of the ritual. '. . . and after the ritual was performed he lay as if dead, and a great lamentation was heard that did shake the walls of the city, a cry that seemed to tear the moon from the sky. Great fear spread through the people, for the stars were darkened and all light was gone from this place.

'But when the holy man awoke, the curse had departed from his soul . . .'

Aduca laid her hand on Venetia's, stilling the tremor in her fingers. 'No one has performed the ritual of curing for hundreds of years,' she said. 'But the Elders have spoken, and we are willing to

195

attempt it.' She turned to Esteban. 'If *you* are willing to risk your life.'

Esteban met her gaze. 'For a vampire, there is no life. Only the darkness and hunger.'

He thought back over seven centuries, seven centuries alone; unchanging, un-ageing. Those who had made him like this had understood, far better than he, that immortality could be the ultimate curse. Immortality, and the hunger that only blood could still . . .

'And you wish to face whatever must be done?'

Taking Aduca's hand, he placed it against his lips. 'I wish to live.'

'You have your life, *Monsieur* Esteban. You have the gift of living forever.'

Esteban's expression darkened. 'All I ask is the chance to live again as other men.'

'There is great risk.'

'I have told you, I will do whatever is necessary.'

'Then you are a brave man, Esteban. Or more foolish than you know.' Aduca looked towards Venetia. 'And you, Venetia. You have read the account of the ceremony. There could be dangers, even for you. You are still willing?'

'I am willing.'

Esteban looked at Aduca sharply. 'You speak of danger – danger to Venetia?'

'She must be by your side during the ceremony. It is through her that the power must be channelled.'

'No!' Esteban pushed Aduca aside and began reading from the ancient book. He grew quiet, his face tense as though he were fighting some inner struggle. At last he looked up. 'This cannot be. I will not allow it.'

Venetia caught his arm. 'It's the only way.'

'I will not risk your life. My life is of no value, it is a living death; but you, Venetia . . . no, not you.'

'I choose to take that risk.' Her voice shook as she realised the implications of what she was saying. Doubt whispered at the back of her mind: do you really care enough? Would he do the same for you?

'And if I refuse to let you?' demanded Esteban.

'You would never refuse me.' She took his fingers and kissed them, one by one. 'Never.'

As she turned back to Aduca, she saw the girl Pernette watching her out of the corner of her eye, sly, half-smiling. No, not watching her; watching *Esteban*. Venetia saw the way her tongue-tip flicked over her lips and jealousy hit her like a kick in the guts.

And yet, what cause had she to be jealous of this half-wild girl and her childish infatuation? Venetia forced herself to look away and question Aduca. 'What must be done?'

'You must spend three days and nights apart. On the night before the ceremony you will be brought together, and that will mark the end of the preparations. The following night . . . if the heavens are willing and the omens are propitious . . .' She clapped her hands and the guards stepped forward. 'Take them away and begin the ceremony of preparation.'

As Venetia was led away, she turned to look back over her shoulder. Pernette was still standing there, that same covetous smile playing about her lips, her dark eyes fixed on Esteban, as though by sheer force of will she could make him desire her as she desired him.

The next three days weighed heavily for Venetia. Forbidden to see Esteban, she found her imagination creating wild scenarios in which things went horribly wrong; scenes of treachery and betrayal; scenes in which she imagined him lying naked with the sly-faced girl Pernette . . .

With difficulty, she forced herself to think sensibly. She was afraid; well, that was only to be expected. She had been forcibly parted from Esteban, inciting her imagination to create monsters which simply didn't exist.

And she longed for Esteban, there was no doubt of that. Through the long nights she lay awake in her cool white-walled cell, gazing up at the star-painted ceiling, imagining she could hear his voice whispering to her on the night-wind: *'Toi seule, Venetia, ma reine, ma destinée . . .* You alone, my destiny, my only one . . .'

In the morning, she went out to explore the city. It quickly became apparent that it consisted of a sequence of rocky chasms, halls and valleys, connected by a maze of tunnels. In the valleys lay beautiful ornamental gardens, wooded glades, orchards and grassy meadows where animals grazed, completely unafraid of their human companions.

She walked through a grove of orange and lemon trees, breathing in the sharp tang of sun-warmed citrus. The fruits hung like luminous globes from the bending branches, reaching themselves into her hands. Everything seemed so peaceful, so perfect. It was difficult to believe that

198

chill darkness could be so very close at hand.

A voice broke into her solitary thoughts. 'You are a difficult woman to find, Venetia Fellowes.'

Aghast, she swung round, her blood turning to ice. Gabriel Engelhart was sitting beneath an orange tree, the girl Pernette crouched in the grass at his feet, her finger stroking his thigh, her face nuzzling into his flesh like a lap-dog's muzzle.

'Gabriel! What the hell are you doing here?'

'Like I told you before, Venetia. Protecting my investment.'

'Leave me alone, I never want to speak to you again.'

'I don't think that's entirely true, Venetia. And you wouldn't want to lie to me, would you? Not after we were so . . . *intimate* together. I mean, I thought we told each other *everything* . . .'

He got to his feet, brushing Pernette aside, and walked alongside Venetia, taking her by the arm and turning her round.

'Don't touch me! Let go . . .'

'Only if you promise not to run away from me.'

'Why the hell should I promise you anything?'

'Because we had an arrangement . . .'

'And you know what you can do with your so-called arrangement.'

'. . . and because I have something very important to say to you.'

'You have nothing to say that I would ever want to hear.'

Pernette caught up with them, stepping in front of Venetia to halt her progress. '*Madame*, I would not be so sure of that.' Her sloe eyes glowed with reflected light.

Venetia looked from Pernette to Gabriel and back again. 'If you're trying to trick me you're not being very subtle about it.'

Gabriel chuckled. An unpleasant sound, thought Venetia – dark and humourless. 'Why be so suspicious, Venetia? Why think the worst of me? Has your lover Esteban made you hate all men . . .?'

'Leave Esteban out of this,' snapped Venetia. Gabriel's expression remained unchanged.

'He is using you, Venetia. He cheated on me and he will betray you too.'

Gabriel's words were like a poisoned dagger in her heart.

'No. I don't believe you, I don't believe any of it.'

Gabriel shook his head. His blond hair, backlit by sunshine, gave the illusion of a pale halo about his face. 'Very well, Venetia, if it is your choice you are free to disbelieve me. But you do so at your peril. Don't you want to know what Esteban is really like? Don't you want to know about the risks you are taking for a man who is scarcely better than a stinking, walking corpse?'

At Gabriel's sign, Pernette began to speak, laying her cool hand on Venetia's.

'*Madame*, I know nothing of Monsieur Esteban,' she began.

Liar, thought Venetia. You know enough about him to want him in your bed, you treacherous little slut.

'. . . But I have heard Baudouin and Aduca speaking of the ritual, and I know what dangers you are to undergo.'

'Listen to her,' said Gabriel, 'and listen well. Her words may save your life, my pretty one.'

Venetia wanted to stop her ears, make it all go away. She wanted to be far, far away from here, on some beach in the South of France, sipping chilled wine and laughing in the sunshine.

'Listen, *madame*. They have told you that the last successful lifting of the blood-curse was many centuries ago. This is true. But what they did not tell you was that there was another attempt, only a few years ago. It went wrong, terribly wrong. The cursed one lived on, but there was also a death, a painful, unspeakable death . . .'

'No . . . No, I won't listen.'

'The Elders have almost forgotten how to use the old wisdom, they scarcely know what they are doing. They will destroy you with their clumsy ignorance. Esteban knows this, but he is willing to risk your life for the chance to save his own . . .'

Venetia lashed out, striking the girl across the face, so hard that it left the imprint of her hand on the tawny features. She sprang back with a hiss of anger and pain.

'How dare you . . . how dare you strike me!'

Venetia's eyes blazed. 'And how dare you tell me these lies?'

'There is no lie . . . it is the truth.' Springing forward, Pernette spat in Venetia's face. 'Only you are too stupid to see it.'

Gabriel seized hold of Pernette and dragged her away. 'Leave her. She will not listen now, but later . . . later she will realise the truth and come running back, begging us to save her.' And later, he thought to himself, I shall have not only Venetia and the *Lore of Madali*, but my sweet, sweet revenge on Esteban.

Venetia wiped her face with an automatic hand. She felt cold, dazed, suddenly frightened. She wished Esteban were here, here to hold her in his arms and tell her that Gabriel's words were lies, vicious, evil lies.

She left Gabriel and Pernette standing in the citrus grove, and walked quickly back towards her room. But try as she might, she could not still the whispering voice in her head.

The voice that whispered darkly of betrayal.

Chapter Twelve

ON THE FOURTH night, Venetia lay in Esteban's arms once more, watching the changing patterns of moonlight play across the mosaic floor of their chamber.

'You are troubled,' he commented, his hand stroking her cheek as they lay together, his naked body strong and hard against the long curve of her backbone.

'No; no it's nothing.' Venetia fought down the fear, but she knew her voice sounded unnaturally quiet and expressionless.

'If it is nothing, why are you afraid?'

'I'm not. I . . .'

He kissed the back of her neck and she shivered, not only with pleasure.

'Petite anglaise, I can smell your fear. I can taste it in your sweat.' He pushed aside the thick curtain of her hair, and dotted tiny kisses between her shoulder blades and up her spine to the base of her skull.

She rolled away from him, afraid of the intensity of sensations he awoke in her. 'It's just

. . . the ritual.' She got to her feet and walked across to the window, resting her arms on the cool, carved stone of the sill.

Esteban rose on one elbow, watching her closely. In the darkness his diamond-black eyes had faded to empty shadows. 'If you are afraid to proceed . . .'

'No. No, of course not.'

'If you are afraid, you have only to say. I swore I would not try to influence you. It is not right that you should face these dangers for my sake.'

She turned round and looked at him. His body was white as sculpted marble in the moonlight. 'I gave my word.'

'And I free you from it.' The word did not come without pain. Venetia felt it shivering through him. 'Gladly.'

'If only I could be sure that that was true.'

He sat up, swinging his legs onto the floor.

'Now I understand.' The realisation hit him, full force. All at once he understood his stupidity. A black, cold feeling of unease had been with him ever since they entered the valley, but he had not been able to identify its cause. He had thought that perhaps the blood-hunger was creeping up on him again. 'It is me that you are afraid of. You don't trust me, do you?'

He took her by the shoulders.

'Please, Esteban . . .' She tried to shrug off his embrace, but he held her fast.

'All I ask is that you tell me why you fear me.'

She avoided his gaze. 'Gabriel Engelhart . . .'

Esteban let go of her, turned and walked away, pacing the room. 'He is here? How could I not have known? And yet, I sensed a darkness growing around this place . . .'

'. . . And that servant-girl, Pernette.'

'She is nothing. A creature of instinct, no more.'

'She is in love with you, I have seen it in her eyes.'

'And you believe . . .?'

'They came to me when I was walking in the orange grove. They spoke to me, told me things, terrible things . . .

Esteban shook his head angrily. 'And poisoned you against me?'

'They spoke of a vampire curing that went very wrong. But that . . . that was not what made me afraid. Gabriel spoke of betrayal. He said you were using me. He said . . . he said you had cheated him, and that in time you would betray me too.'

Esteban sank down onto the bed. 'I see. And you believe this?'

'I don't know what to believe.'

'No. I suppose not.' He looked up. 'Are you in love with Gabriel Engelhart.'

'I despise him, you know that. But . . .'

'But he has placed doubt in your mind, and you cannot drive it out.' He ran his fingers through his hair. 'What is it you wish from me, Venetia?'

'The truth. That's all I ask.'

'Gabriel Engelhart is the essence of purest evil. That, *ma petite anglaise*, is the truth.'

He saw Venetia open her mouth to speak, and hushed her with a gesture of his hand. 'But I do not expect you to believe that, and I cannot prove it to you. However, I will tell you why I hate and despise him.

'Fifteen years ago, Gabriel Engelhart had nothing. He was a penniless art student who sold his body to rich old women for the price of a meal. That is how he came to Valazur, as the companion of an elderly countess who liked to flatter herself by having a young man on her arm.

'I disliked him the first time I saw him. Two years later, when we met again, I had grown to loathe him. Engelhart had become phenomenally, inexplicably successful in those two years. He was a millionaire now, a dilettante and a seducer. A cold-eyed, ruthless wheeler-dealer whose greatest pleasures were money and the corruption of innocence. I knew the first time I looked into his eyes that I was looking upon a vision of chaos and evil.

'At that time on the Riviera, there were rumours . . . stories that Engelhart had dabbled in the black arts, that this was how he had come by such riches and success. He roused my curiosity, and I made it my business to find out more about him. The stories, Venetia . . . they were all true. Gabriel Engelhart had been playing with fire and he was about to get burned.'

Venetia hardly knew what to say or do. 'And you expect me to believe that Gabriel Engelhart is some kind of black magician?'

Esteban laughed drily. 'From you, *chère petite anglaise*, I expect nothing, except that you will listen and judge me on my words. Gabriel Engelhart was and is a fool, an amateur, a dabbler in matters he could neither understand nor control. Another, far more powerful and more malevolent, manipulated Engelhart's greed, trapped him into a bargain; Engelhart would receive all the riches a man could desire, in return for . . .'

'His soul?' enquired Venetia ironically.

'Sometimes, *ma petite*, the incredible and the ridiculous can be true. Yes, *chère anglaise*, his soul. His immortal soul, which was trapped by magic inside a mirror . . .'

'But Esteban . . .'

'Trapped within a mirror which was later shattered, and the soul lost for ever, never to be regained. Not that it troubled Gabriel Engelhart that he had become a man without a soul. It only served to make his life easier, robbed him of the tiresome inhibitions which had impeded him for so long. Now, he could do anything he desired, and never be troubled by conscience.

'But there was still one thing that Gabriel Engelhart craved. The gift of immortality. And unfortunately Engelhart had discovered the truth about me, about the curse which binds me to this earth.

'He came to me one night, begged me, pleaded with me to give him what he craved. To drink his life-blood and make him a vampire.'

'And you . . .?'

'Naturally I refused. He grew violent, trying to provoke me, blackmail me, threaten me, knowing the strength of the black hunger within me. But still I refused him. I told him in no uncertain terms that I despised him, that such a man as he was unworthy. I would not sully my lips with his filthy blood.'

He smiled in the darkness.

'And so it is that he and I became enemies. I always suspected that Gabriel Engelhart's resentment would drive him to the ends of the earth to destroy me; and as you see, he has followed me even here.'

'Surely he came here because he wants the *Lore of Madali*.'

'No doubt he would risk a great deal to own a book of such esoteric power. But he would risk everything to see me cursed to eternal damnation.'

Venetia thought she could hear Esteban's heart thumping in the silence.

'Why didn't you tell me this before?'

'It served no purpose.'

'No purpose!' Anger quickened in Venetia. 'You knew about Gabriel, and you just let me . . .'

Esteban put up his hand. 'I followed you Venetia, don't you remember? You were angry with me for knowing so much about you, for interfering in your life when I had sworn to leave it forever. But I had been watching over you, Venetia, watching over you these last two years, though always at a distance. I swore to you that I would let you have your freedom . . . but equally, I would never let any harm come to you. Never. And that is why I cannot ask you to risk your life for me.'

He reached out and drew her to him. She felt the coolness of his breath on her cheek, yearned for him, felt her passion opening up to him. And she knew that, despite her fear, despite Engelhart's talk of betrayal, she believed him. That she would risk anything for a chance to be with him.

'You don't have to ask me.' She kissed him, her passion taking over, guiding her lips and her hands. She smoothed her fingers over the sharp contours of his face, the long sweep of neck and back, the hardness of buttock and thigh.

They sank down together to their knees, facing

each other on the cool mosaic floor. Esteban murmured to her as his fingers caressed the upturned points of her breasts. *'Ma reine, ma reine de la nuit* . . . my queen of darkness, you excite me, you rouse me to sweet madness . . .'

As they rolled on the floor, their limbs entwined, they breathed in the sweet, musky fragrance of damask roses.

'You are my temptation, my obsession . . .'

Venetia scarcely knew if she was really hearing Esteban's words, or if she was listening to his thoughts. She felt as though she had entered the secret rhythm of his being, his hunger joining hers and making her mad for him, animal-hungry for his body.

He lay behind her, the throbbing lance of his manhood pulsing as it pushed into the valley between her buttocks. She had to have him, could not wait any longer, had to feel him inside her.

'Take me,' she gasped. And she thrust back with a single flex of her hips, opening herself, taking the tip of his cock and swallowing it up in the haven of her sex.

Esteban responded with a long thrust. Venetia cried out as she felt his thick cock-ring distending the walls of her pussy, driving deep into her, seeking out the supersensitive G-spot at the front of her vagina and caressing it with a brutal tenderness.

'Oh yes, Esteban, oh yes . . .' She held apart her buttocks, urging him deeper, and he pushed hard into her until his heavy seed-sacs were slapping against the juicy split fig of her sex.

They coupled with the madness of lovers who know there may not be much more time; lovers who live for the moment, for the exquisite power of the passion which drives them on.

Moving her hips, Venetia drove back again and again onto Esteban's prick. He slid one hand onto her breast, the other down into the soft dark tangle of her maidenhair, winding his fingers about the honeyblonde curls, letting a fingertip stray lower, to the pout of her labia, to the tingling, juice-filled flowerstalk within.

It could not last long; it was too powerful, a meeting not only of bodies but of spirits. A lightning-flash of pleasure; a short, savage spasm that tore through him, and then it was gone, leaving them exhausted, spent, their bodies tangled in the warm, sweat-scented aftermath of pleasure.

Esteban stroked the side of Venetia's face as she slept in the crook of his arm. He had expressed his passion towards her, but he could not express the fear. The fear that he had brought her into his own private nightmare, into a world which might yet destroy them both.

Silently, he lay down beside her and watched the sky grow light. Waiting for the day to begin.

As the sun set once more over Tamezion, and darkness crept down over the mountains, a strange, expectant silence fell over the city.

Esteban and Venetia, dressed in high-collared ceremonial robes of unbleached linen, were led along a narrow, winding passageway towards the distant glow of flickering flame.

They emerged into a high-walled courtyard lined with polished black stone, the floor strewn ankle-deep with great drifts of white lilies and orchids. Bonfires in iron braziers stood at each corner, their flames licking with yellow and red tongues at the heavy, blue-black darkness, and the air was heavy with the scent of incense and fragrant woods. High above hung the round, yellow disc of the full moon.

Aduca stepped forward. 'You are willing?'

'We are willing.'

'Then the ritual may begin.'

Somewhere in the distance, Venetia heard the slow thump, thump, thump of a hundred drums, beating in unison. Her heart raced in double time, skipping beats; her mouth dry, her throat hoarse. The low hum of a distant, mumbled chant filled her head, making her dizzy and disorientated. She looked at Esteban. His face was expressionless, but his skin felt clammy and cold.

'Let darkness fall.'

At the word from Aduca, the bonfires were extinguished, one by one; scented smoke filled the courtyard as water sizzled on the embers. As darkness crept over them, Venetia heard Esteban's voice in her head: 'You alone, *petite anglaise*. You alone.'

Her last glimpse was of a face in the crowd. A face she loathed, despised and feared. The face of Gabriel Engelhart, smiling at her as if he knew some obscene secret . . .

She put Gabriel's face out of her mind. Perhaps he had been there, perhaps not. She might easily have imagined his evil smile, creeping into her consciousness to destroy her. She must remember what she had been told, the precise order of the ceremonial.

In the darkness, she felt unseen hands

stripping her, unfastening and peeling away the robe. The night air felt cold on her bare skin. Then something cold, wet; soft sable brushes painting her body with secret signs, signs so powerful that they could only be drawn in darkness, where none but the eye of heaven could see them. That was what Aduca had said. Venetia wondered, with a frisson of fear, if any of this was real, true; if Gabriel Engelhart could even have been right . . .

The hands slipped away and the drums began to quicken; the beat faster, faster, louder until it became a blur of sound.

They knew what they must do now.

Venetia and Esteban drew together, nakedness meeting nakedness in the darkness. The scents of sweet unguents dripped and melted from their bodies as they embraced. Closer, closer, closer. And kissed.

As their mouths met the whole world seemed to tremble. From somewhere nearby – or was it a thousand miles away? – Venetia heard a shrill cry, then silence.

Closer, closer, tighter; two becoming one, the passion growing, the hunger shared and burning.

Until at last, a bright light burst in the sky above them, showering down upon them, glowing with a furnace-heat which descended to earth, enshrouding and enveloping them.

Hiding them from human sight.

Esteban stirred. He groaned with pain as he opened his eyes; his whole body felt bruised and painfully sensitive.

It was daylight, and reflexively he narrowed his

eyes, waiting for the sear of discomfort; but it did not come. His body welcomed the brightness, the warmth, the daylight. His heart thumped. A change had come upon him, he felt . . . different. Could it be true? Or was he dreaming it all, only to awaken in some other place at some other time, to discover that he was still Esteban? Esteban the vampire.

Slowly and dizzily he sat up, and took a look around him. He saw that he was no longer in the black courtyard, not even in Tamezion. He was back in the wooded valley he and Venetia had explored, close by the gateway to the city.

Venetia. Where was Venetia? Panic grabbed at his guts. She was there, he could see her; but she was lying sprawled face-down on the earth, her honeygold hair spreading out around her in damp, disarrayed tendrils. She was not moving.

He tried to stand, but felt much too weak, all his accustomed strength drained from him, fear invading him as it had not for over seven hundred years. He stretched out his hand to touch her.

'Venetia . . . His voice was scarcely more than a dry croak. Still Venetia did not move; she just lay there, pallid, unmoving, her skin deathly cold.

Mocking laughter rang out behind Esteban. He turned to see Gabriel Engelhart, arms folded, head thrown back in vicious merriment.

'I have waited too long for this moment, Esteban,' he smirked. 'You were fools to trust the people of the city and their pathetic "wisdom". And I fear you have underestimated me. It was obvious to me from the beginning that the Englishwoman was the only thing you have ever cared about, beyond yourself. And it was simplicity itself to seduce Pernette and have her alter the words of the ancient ritual so that your precious Venetia would be destroyed. Now the *Lore of Madali* is mine, the English bitch is dead, and you and I are equals.' He chuckled to himself. 'Though I scarcely see you as my equal, Esteban; poor, feeble, half-dead creature that you are.'

Esteban snarled his defiance, but his weakened body would not obey him, and as he lunged in rage towards Gabriel, his old enemy kicked out, catching him in the belly and sending him spinning to the ground, sick and helpless. Engelhart stood over Esteban, the smile never leaving his lips.

'What is it, my old friend? Are you too much of a coward to fight me now that your powers have left you?'

Panting, struggling for breath, Esteban looked up at Gabriel through eyes that swore vengeance. 'You are the devil incarnate.'

'And you, my dear Esteban, are a pathetic fool. For only a fool would choose mortality over eternal life.' His boot slid over Esteban's outstretched hand, and exerted pressure slowly and deliciously, crushing it into the dusty earth. 'How do you like your new life, Esteban? Such a pity that it will be so brief. But I shall do what I can to give you an interesting death . . .'

As Esteban's face contorted in helpless pain, his half-closed eyes made out a sudden shape . . . a lithe and savage thing that leaped and sprang. A creature of claws and teeth, that growled and hissed as it dragged Engelhart away and flung him to the ground.

'Venetia . . .' gasped Esteban, as Gabriel Engelhart fell away from him with a curse of pain, blood springing crimson from his bitten throat. 'Venetia, *petite anglaise*, what curse have I inflicted upon your sweet flesh?'

It was much later, and Venetia was sitting, cross-legged, upon the ground. Night had fallen in the valley, and a sweet languor had fallen over everything, the perfumed air soft and gentle, and quiet with the soft whisperings of a thousand night-creatures. Death had no place here, and yet Gabriel Engelhart was very dead.

Esteban lay beside her, his sleeping face pale in the moonlight; his dark hair falling across his cheek in a sweat-moistened strand. Tenderly she brushed it aside. He stirred briefly in his dream but she willed him not to wake, and he slumbered on, the darkness cradling him in its warm embrace.

When dawn broke, they would head back through the mountains together, leaving Engelhart's body sprawled on the ground beside the stolen book which had brought nothing but destruction; and before the gateway to the city of Tamezion. The gateway, which by some mystery had closed forever, reduced to a few ancient and meaningless carvings on a sheer rock face.

She knew it had gone for all eternity. Like her own mortality.

Venetia looked down at Esteban, her passion for him both savage and tender. Her life for his, it had seemed a small price to pay, but after all, she had not died. She had taken his darkness upon her and lived on, cursed as he had been cursed. A vampire now, as Esteban had been before.

She stroked her long, slender fingers over his neck and shoulder. He was beautiful. She longed to nuzzle against his throat and sip the elixir of his life-blood. But she could never harm him. She adored him with a passion that transcended simple hunger.

And so she would sit beside him through the night, and guard him. And in the morning they would travel on together. Into the unknown.

Epilogue

THE MEDITERRANEAN SURF crashed on the beach, far below.

In the grounds of Esteban's villa, high above the sea, two figures walked amid the orange trees.

'I have betrayed you, *petite anglaise,*' said Esteban, gazing out to sea, watching the pinks and apricots of dawn slowly blooming in the royal-blue sky.

'It was my choice to take the risk. You know that, Esteban.'

He turned to look at her, the old fire burning deep in his glittering dark eyes.

'If I had known. If I had known that this might happen, I would not have permitted it . . .'

Venetia flicked back her long mane of blonde hair. 'You could not have known, nobody could.'

'And Engelhart's treachery . . .'

She looked him in the eyes.

'Gabriel Engelhart is dead.'

'Yes.'

'Can you forgive me?'

'For saving me? For taking his foul and useless

life? There is nothing to forgive, Venetia.' He took her hand. 'If not for you, I would be dead.'

Venetia returned his gaze, her blue eyes bright. 'I don't regret what has happened to me, and neither must you.'

He laughed bitterly. 'But I have placed a curse upon you. A terrible hunger, a darkness that will abide with you for ever . . .'

'Eternity is a long time, Esteban. There will be other chances, we will find other ways to make things right. I am content. Or at least, I am patient. I can wait.'

Esteban took both her hands in his.

'We might both be content, *petite anglaise*,' he whispered. 'There could be a way . . .'

Venetia shivered, suddenly cold. She knew what he was thinking. Hadn't she thought it herself, a thousand times these last weeks?

'No, Esteban . . .'

'You have the power, Venetia. It is within you now. Will you deny me what I once offered you?'

'Esteban, you're crazy. I won't do it . . .'

He hushed her with a kiss, his warmth and urgency melting the fear that lapped at the edges of her mind. She felt his heart thumping against her chest, felt the tremor of excitement pass through him. And his excitement aroused her, the tang of his sweat, the animal warmth making her hunger for him in a hundred dark and dangerous ways. She let out a low moan of longing.

'Venetia. Listen to me. Once, long ago, I offered you immortality. Now I am asking you to bestow the same upon me.'

She stared back at him, at once incredulous and excited. 'You're asking me . . . you want to become a vampire again? After all these hundreds of years of searching . . .? Esteban, you are mortal again, you have what you wanted . . .'

'I do not have you.'

'Leave, Esteban. Leave Valazur, you can go anywhere now, be anything, love any mortal woman . . .'

'It is you I want, Venetia.'

'If you stay with me, there is such danger. You, of all men, know the darkness and the hunger . . .'

His eyes met hers, their gaze steady and strong. 'Can it be danger if it is something I truly crave?'

They walked on through the trees, the lawns gradually sloping down to the cliff edge. Behind them, the stone turrets of the villa rose up to puncture the lightening sky, letting in the sun. Beneath them, the distant surf crashed down on the beach, spray framing a lone figure walking along the margin of the sea, picking up driftwood.

'It will soon be light, Venetia.'

'I know.'

'It should be now.' He took her hand and drew her down beside him on the dew-fresh grass, scented, cool and moist. 'Now, Venetia. Kiss me now.'

Their lips met, their hands roaming over each other's bodies, the old hunger meeting the new, the darkness battling the light. Venetia pulled away.

'No, Esteban. I can't do this . . .'

'For me, Venetia. Do this because you hunger for me, as I hunger for you.'

Venetia closed her eyes. A red mist cloaked her vision, her pulse raced, a black hunger filling her, overtaking her, mingling passion and tenderness and savage need.

And her lips brushed Esteban's throat. He tasted salty, appetising, the blood pulsing softly in a fat vein, just beneath the skin.

'For ever, Esteban. You are sure?'

'For ever.'

'Venetia . . . aah . . .'

Esteban let out the softest sigh of orgasm as her teeth broke the skin of his throat. Venetia drank deeply, a strange exhilaration filling her as their passion joined and pleasure refreshed her insatiable, immortal, incorruptible body.

Afterwards, she laid him down tenderly on the grass, in the shade of tall pines, and lay beside him, curling around and about him, her face snuggled into the crook of his neck and her lips still moist with the taste of him.

Death would claim him for a few hours, no more. And when night came and he awoke, they would be together again.

Together for all eternity.